The Baby Bargain

The Billionaire's Baby, Volume 1

Ellis O. Day

Published by L. S. O'Dea, 2021.

This is a work of fiction. Similarities to real people, places, or events are entirely coincidental.

THE BABY BARGAIN

First edition. May 23, 2021.

Copyright © 2021 Ellis O. Day.

ISBN: 979-8201857479

Written by Ellis O. Day.

CHAPTER 1: Harker

Harker glanced at his watch. Alison was late. Again. She was the most brilliant woman he'd ever met but she needed to work on her punctuality. "Alison!" he yelled.

"Don't bellow at her. She's not your dog." Merri sat across from him at the table in his office looking as perfectly put together as always.

They'd been friends since junior high and she never had a hair out of place. She looked like a blonde cover girl model, but it'd always been her kindness and intelligence that'd attracted him. She'd fallen for his college roommate, Tobias, and that'd been the end of Harker's infatuation with Merri. Even back then he'd known that it wasn't worth losing the only two friends he had over a one-sided crush.

"I know she's not my dog, but she's late." He'd like her to be his sub, but he had more important plans for her. "Alison, get in here now!"

"She's getting your lunch." Merri sent him a disgusted look. "Stop yelling. She'll be here when she's done."

"Did he yell? I thought that was his normal tone." Alison swooped into his office like a refreshing breeze.

Harker swore the energy in the room crackled whenever Alison was in it. She was a whirlwind of movement, both her body and her mouth. The first time he'd met her he'd been fascinated by the barrage of words that'd flowed effortlessly from her lips. They were both rambling and humorous. He'd become even more fascinated over the months that he'd known her, always waiting to see what odd or inappropriate thing would come from her soft pink lips.

Alison dropped a wrapped deli sub, a bag of chips and a can of cola in front of Merri. "That's the only tone he ever uses around me."

"Maybe if you were on time, I wouldn't." Most people, besides Merri and Tobias, treated him with deference because of his wealth but not Alison. She didn't seem to care about his money or power. It annoyed and excited him.

"Please." Her brown eyes sparkled with amusement. "You scream at me when I'm in my office and I'm not late then. I'm working." She dug in the bag from the deli.

"I do not scream." He held out his hand. He was starving. "Screaming implies hysterics and I'm never hysterical."

"You can say that again. Dour is more like it." She dropped a wrapped sub in his hand and then put a water and a bag of apple slices on his desk.

"He was even dour in college." Merri laughed.

"I was not. I was serious and hard-working. We wouldn't have this business if I hadn't been."

"Tobias and I worked hard too." Merri opened her bag of chips. "But we also knew how to have fun." Her eyes met his and then darted to Alison who was seated across the table with her lunch in front of her.

He gave Merri a glare and shook his head. She'd noticed his interest in Alison and had mentioned, more times than he could count, that he should ask her out. What Merri didn't understand and what he couldn't tell her was that he had no plans on dating Alison. He had another arrangement in mind that would be beneficial to both of them. All he had to do was find the right time to make her the offer. It may require a little persuading at first, but he'd convince her. He always figured out a way to get what he wanted.

Alison opened her bag of chips. "Speaking of having fun. I'm going on a—"

"Where are my chips? And why do I have water? I want a soda."

"Because you need to start eating better." Alison chomped on a chip. "You're not a young man anymore. You have to watch your cholesterol and blood pressure."

"I'm not old." That was so insulting. "I'm in great shape." He worked out every day and saw women, young women, checking him out all the time.

"You said your blood pressure was high. Chips are loaded with salt and that's not good for high blood pressure."

"My blood pressure is high because you drive me crazy."

"Me?" She pointed at herself. "What do I do?"

"Do you really want me to start? It's a long list." He unwrapped his sandwich. "What's this? It's not what I ordered." It was full of vegetables.

"It is what you ordered. Roast beef."

He stared at the sandwich and opened it slowly not wanting to see what vegetables she'd had them add.

"It's not going to bite you," said Alison.

"I'm well aware of that."

"Then why are you opening it like it's going to attack you?" She tried and failed to keep the laughter out of her voice.

Normally, he loved her sense of humor. She could find fun in anything but not when she was torturing him. "Why did you do this to me?" He looked at her. "I'm a good guy. I pay you well."

"They're vegetables, not poison." She rolled her eyes at him.

"I hate tomatoes."

"There are no tomatoes on there even though I can't understand how anyone can hate tomatoes." She sighed pulling one from her sandwich and biting into it. "They are so yummy and good for you."

The look of pure satisfaction on her face made the blood rush to his cock. He wanted her looking at him like that after he made her come or better yet, when she had his dick in her mouth. Shit. She had him wanting to be a fucking tomato.

"But it's fine if you don't like them. To each his own and all that." She waved her sandwich at him. "I had them add extra green peppers. You like those."

He almost groaned as she pulled another tomato from her sandwich and licked the mayonnaise off it. Merri snorted.

He tore his gaze away from Alison and gave Merri a quick "shut up" look. "I do like green peppers but why is there so much lettuce. I didn't order a salad."

"You should've," Alison muttered around a bite of her sandwich.

"I may as well have. I can barely see the meat. This is not double meat. I like double meat."

"Meat isn't good for you, especially deli meat. It's full of nitrates, fat and sodium."

"There's no cheese." He picked at the vegetables.

"Your cholesterol." Alison turned toward Merri. "Does he know nothing about health?"

"He's a man. Men think they can continue to eat like they're in their twenties and they're too stubborn to listen to good advice...about a lot of things." Merri gave him an exasperated look before glancing at Alison.

"I know about health and I don't have high cholesterol. Why do you think I do?" Talking to Alison was like mental calisthenics.

"You said you were going to have a heart attack." Alison took a big bite of her sandwich, trying to look innocent.

"I never..." He was going to strangle her. "I said that because you make me crazy and you're going to give me a heart attack, not because I have high cholesterol." He snatched her bag of chips.

"Hey, those are mine."

"You should've gotten me chips instead of these." He tossed the apples at her.

"I'm not the one complaining about my blood pressure and my heart." She threw the apples across the desk, smacking him in the chest. "Give me back my chips."

"No"—he leaned forward and dumped them in the middle of the table—"but I'll share."

"They're my chips," she huffed as she took one. "You have apples."

"I'll share those too." He opened the bag and dropped them in the middle of the table next to the chips. "And I'll forgive you for the shitty sandwich." He closed it and took a bite.

"I'm not apologizing." She sent him a challenging look. "You should be thanking me. Vegetables are good for you."

"So is squashing impertinence." He frowned at her. "But we can talk about that later. Now, let's hear how the facial recognition enhancement is going with my software." He stressed the word "my" because it annoyed the shit out of her. He loved watching her bristle and struggle to keep from arguing with him. He was pretty sure that one day she was going to go off like a hot tea kettle.

She'd spent countless hours writing this code. It was more hers than his, except he owned it. He'd leverage that possessiveness of hers to get what he wanted.

She was young, in good health, extremely intelligent and for some reason his cock wanted her like it hadn't wanted anyone since he'd been a horny teenager. He'd weighed all the pros and cons and had decided that she was the perfect woman to bear his child.

CHAPTER 2: Alison

Alison finished giving Merri and Harker the update on her progress. She was proud of this. This program was hers. She'd taken the shell from a previous programmer and had expanded on it, making it unique.

"That's amazing. No, you're amazing." Merri smiled at Alison. "You're way ahead of schedule."

"Thank you." Alison glanced at Harker.

He stared at his computer, the glow from the screen making the smattering of gray at his temples shine almost silver in his dark hair. She should be used to his reticence by now but for some reason it hurt her feelings. She didn't need someone to praise her all the time, but she worked hard for this man—long hours, holidays, weekends—and he barely ever acknowledged her accomplishments.

"We should celebrate." Merri sent a cautious glance toward Harker.

Alison had noticed the many quiet exchanges between the two tonight. She wondered again if they were having an affair. She had to grind her teeth together to keep her big mouth shut. Tobias adored his wife and didn't deserve to be treated this way.

"The four of us should go out." Merri grabbed her phone. "I'll call Tobias and—"

"Alison, do you think you can have a demo ready next week?" Harker continued to stare at his laptop.

"A canned demo? Sure. I can modify the one we made for the initial funding and prep the screenshots and—"

"No. Live." He tapped his screen. "I'm sure I can get a meeting arranged—"

"Live? Next week? You mean like we'll scan someone's face and watch it work?"

"Exactly." His dark eyes met hers over his laptop. "Is that a problem? From what you claimed in this meeting it shouldn't be an issue."

"I said several core components were done but they've never been linked together and tested."

"Then link them and test it."

"I will." Now, she remembered why she hated this job as much as she loved it. Him. This man was never satisfied.

"By Wednesday."

"No. That's not possible."

"That's five days from now. Seems more than possible to me."

"Five? No." She shook her head. "I have this weekend off, remember?"

"Plans change." His lips turned up in a half-smirk.

"Harker," Merri scolded him. "We agreed that Alison could have this weekend off. We're not making her work."

She bit the inside of her mouth to keep from pointing out that she shouldn't have to get approval to have a weekend off.

"I agreed to that before I had all the data." Harker leaned back in his chair.

"I'm being punished for getting things done early?" This man was unbelievable. Every freaking time she thought she knew how much of a jerk he could be, he surprised her in a horrible way.

"If you think working here is a punishment"—his eyes darkened and dipped for a moment—"you have no idea what punishment is."

If she didn't know better, she would've sworn he'd looked at her breasts. Of course, that'd be a joke because first, her breasts had never drawn a man's gaze and second, Harker wasn't a man. Not really. He was a boss. A machine that did nothing but work.

"Enough." Merri stood. "We can all use the weekend off and we can discuss the project timeline on Monday. Admit it, Harker. A night out with just the four of us will be fun. We'll eat, have some drinks, dance. Get to know each other better."

There was that secret undertone again. Alison wasn't going to be the decoy to keep Tobias entertained while these two fooled around right in front of his face.

"I suppose it can wait a night." He frowned, his dark gaze on her again. "Make the arrangements. Alison and I will meet you and Tobias later tonight."

"Tonight?" Even after working for him for almost a year, the intensity of his gaze still made her uncomfortable. It was like he was studying her, analyzing her and she had no idea why. Men never studied her. Most males barely gave her a second glance. She wasn't particularly attractive. Her hair was long and brown with a tendency to frizz in the humidity. She was tall and on the thin side. Her breasts were small and her face, while not unattractive, wasn't anything that'd make anyone take a second look. She often thought she should've been a spy because people never really saw her. Unfortunately, her tendency to yammer on about everything had killed those dreams.

However, for some odd reason, Harker looked at her. He saw her. He didn't seem to know what to make of her but at least he looked. That was probably why she'd stayed at this job. He was arrogant, demanding and could be a jerk but she liked him. Plus, the money was really good.

"Yes, tonight." He watched her as if she were a bug under a glass.

"Sorry. I can't tonight." She liked her job, but she needed more than work. She needed a life and a man. It'd been way too long since she'd had sex. "Maybe tomorrow."

"Why can't you join us for dinner tonight?" He closed his laptop.

"Because I have a date." She grinned like a fool. She was so excited. She probably wouldn't get laid tonight but if things went well with Randy the possibility of sex was in her future again.

CHAPTER 3: Harker

"A date?" Merri's eyes widened and she glanced at Harker. "That's wonderful. Who is he? Where did you meet. This is so exciting. Tell me everything about this mystery man."

Normally, Harker would've wanted to wipe that smirk from Merri's face but today the only thing going through his mind was, *Hell no. The future mother of his child was not going out and getting laid by some strange dick.* He'd tie her to his bed before he let that happen. His cock rose at the thought of Alison restrained, looking up at him, licking those pink lips but his dick deflated as she began talking.

"His name is Randy." She almost vibrated with excitement. "He finally asked me out. We met online a few weeks ago and we've been video chatting. He's so nice. He's an architect and shy and..."

Alison's brown eyes sparkled, and her smile was wide and natural. The blood rushed back to his dick. He'd never noticed how wide her mouth was. Probably because she never smiled like that for him, but she would. He almost groaned as he imagined her on her knees, smiling up at him before she opened that big mouth of hers and swallowed his cock.

"So, you're looking forward to this date?" Merri gave him an I-told-you-so look.

He ignored her and shifted slightly, trying to tamp down his desire. He was forty years old not some teenage boy with no control over his dick.

"Where are the two of you going?" asked Merri.

"Nowhere." He didn't even flinch as both women fell silent and turned, staring at him. Merri had an amused expression on her face, but Alison was surprised. Too bad. She'd surprised him with the news of this date. He'd thought they'd spent almost every waking moment together for almost a year but apparently, she'd found some time to video chat with some ass-wipe named Randy. "You're not going on this date."

"Excuse me?" Alison's tone held a hint of warning.

He ignored it. "You heard me." He put his hand on his computer. "There's work to do."

"Not for me. I have the weekend off."

"Not any longer." He wasn't letting her out of his sight. He wasn't risking her womb being infiltrated by this other man's sperm.

"We just discussed this. I have the weekend off. You can't change your mind." She glanced at Merri for help, but the other woman remained silent, watching them like they were her favorite TV show.

"I can. I'm the boss." He was growing tired of her constant resistance to his authority.

"I've worked every weekend for the last ten months. I come in early and work late every day. All I do is work."

"I know. You've proven that you're smart and dedicated. You know that when there's work to be done sacrifices are made. Which is why I'm confused that you still think you're going on a date tonight." He almost snarled at the thought of her sitting and chatting with some stranger. The man touching her. Kissing her. Fuck, that was so not going to happen. She was his. He'd found her and chosen her.

"I'm going because you gave me the weekend off. Which I shouldn't have had to ask for. It's the weekend. I've already worked over eighty hours this week."

"As have I."

"It's your company."

"Good. You understand." He leaned forward. "I'm your boss."

"You're an ass."

He tipped his head in agreement. "When I have to be."

"Well, Gus—" She leaned toward him.

"Don't call me that." His words were soft, a warning.

"Harker." Merri's tone was cautious. She knew him well enough to know he was one whisper away from exploding.

"I'm not working this weekend, Gus." Alison glared at him.

She should know better than to push him, but he'd never had to show her this side of him. She'd always obeyed—with a snarky attitude many times but she'd bowed to his demands like a good sub. No, she wasn't his sub and she'd never be his sub. She was a good employee and soon she'd be a good mother, but that was it. "You are working this weekend and if you call me Gus one more time, I'll—"

"Harker don't." Merri stood. "Let's everyone take a deep breath and we can talk about this like adults."

"There's nothing to discuss." He was the boss. He'd made his decision and Alison would just have to deal with it.

"On that we agree." Alison picked up her laptop. "I'll see you on Monday."

"If you leave, you're fired."

"Harker." Merri turned to Alison. "Please give me a minute with him."

Alison nodded and strode out of the room.

CHAPTER 4: Harker

Harker wasn't backing down on this. Alison wasn't going on a date. "There is nothing you can say Merri—"

Merri closed the door and spun around. "You can't order her around like that. She's not your sub."

"I'm well aware of what she is. She'd make a horrible sub." But she'd be fun to train—all that energy, the attitude. He'd never be able to fully make her submit and that'd make each tiny submission mean that much more. He frowned, reminding himself that he wasn't looking for a sub. He was looking for someone with good genes to mix with his. "But she is my employee."

"Who you've overworked for months. The hours that woman puts in is crazy."

"She's well compensated—"

"Money isn't everything, Harker."

"I'm aware of that." But it did get him everything he needed.

"I don't think you are." Merri shook her head at him. "You can't fire her."

"I can. I hired her—"

"I hired her."

"Semantics." He shrugged. "I approved it and she works for me. For my department. I can fire her."

"Stop acting like an ass and tell her how you feel."

"Feel?" He rolled his eyes. "This has nothing to do with feelings." It had to do with keeping her untainted to ensure that the child that'd soon be in her womb would be his.

"Please. You're always watching her, and you make her work every day, even holidays. You keep her here until all hours of the night. You make her come into work instead of telecommuting like almost every other employee."

"She needs to be here. We can't risk the program getting stolen." He was glad when Merri ignored him because they both knew that he had enough funds to minimize that risk to almost nothing.

"You even gave her a room in your house. Not in the business side of your mansion but in your home. A room right down the hallway from yours."

"And would I do that if I had *feelings* for her?" He'd considered asking her to join him in his bedroom on several occasions, especially the ones where he'd heard her moving about in her bed, soft little sighs and a low hum coming from the room. It'd taken every bit of willpower he had not to barge in there and let her use his cock instead of that stupid toy, but no matter how much he'd wanted that, she was too important for a heated fling.

"I'm not sure why you haven't slept with her when it's obvious to anyone with eyes that you want her."

"It's not sexual between us." Yes, they'd be having sex, but not for pleasure. Of course, there was no reason not to make it pleasurable. Some studies suggested that pleasure assisted in the likelihood of conceiving. Plus, pregnancy didn't usually occur the first time. Even if it did, it'd take several weeks to know for sure and he planned on using those weeks and Alison quite thoroughly.

"Really?" Her eyebrow raised. "This power thing has always been your aphrodisiac."

"Not with Alison. Like I said. She'd make an awful sub."

"Then why are you doing this?" She studied him. "It's clear you're attracted to her."

"I suppose I am. To her mind."

"Her mind?"

"Yes." That wasn't a lie. Alison was the most intelligent woman he'd ever met, and she was more logical than most, not prone to making decisions on emotions.

"Then tell her."

"I plan to."

"When?"

He shrugged. "When it's time." He had to play his cards right because he didn't want to start this new project with an angry and unwilling partner. He'd get Alison to agree to his deal one way or another, but he preferred bribery over blackmail.

"The right time is now. The poor woman hasn't done anything but work for almost a year."

"Obviously, that's incorrect because she found time to video chat with Randy." He couldn't keep the venom from his voice.

"Harker tell her how you feel. Take her to dinner or a movie."

"I don't want to date her."

"Then what do you want?"

"That's between me and her." He was in no mood to hear Merri's opinion on his plan. She wouldn't be a fan.

"If you're too stubborn to tell her how you feel about her—"

"I feel nothing for her except admiration for her brain." He'd always been drawn to smart women. Usually, they were more physically attractive than Alison, but he never argued with his dick. He just gave it what it wanted.

"Then you and your admiration will have to accept the fact that she's going to date other men."

"She isn't." He couldn't allow that.

"She is and you're not going to fire her over it."

"Of course not."

Merri sighed in relief and he wanted to laugh.

"That would be unethical. I am, however, going to fire her if she doesn't work this weekend, including tonight."

"I have no idea why I waste my time with you about anything that has to do with feelings."

"Me either. You've known me for over twenty-five years. You should know I'm never swayed by emotions."

"That's right." Merri smiled and Harker's instincts screamed a warning. "Let me speak to your logical side. You can't fire her because without her, your application won't get finished and you'll have no product for all those investors."

"I'll hire someone else."

"That didn't work before."

"You were in the meeting. She's solved most of the issues with performance. The facial recognition is the next big hurdle and she's having some problems getting that to work. I already have a few candidates in mind."

"You'd fire her and hand this over to someone else? After all the work she's done?" Merri stared at him with disbelief. "I know you can be ruthless, but until now you've always been fair."

"And I'll be fair to her too." He was going to be more than fair. He was going to offer her the one thing she wanted most in the world and all it'd cost her was the use of her womb.

"You can't keep her as your slave. Consent is always the rule. You know that."

"That's with sex."

"That's with everything."

"Don't worry. I have no intention of forcing her to do anything." He grinned. "Alison will consent. She'll stay and work."

"I don't know, Harker. I think you may have pushed her too far."

"Trust me. I know Alison and I know what I'm doing." He was an expert at recognizing what a person wanted and what they'd do to get it. It'd been the only way he'd survived in foster care. Alison may not be a true sub, but she liked her job and she liked to please. She'd give in to his demands like always.

CHAPTER 5: Alison

Alison paced in her office. She wasn't working tonight. She'd done everything Harker had asked her to do—late nights, weekends, holidays—but that stopped now. She hadn't had a date in over a year, and it'd been longer since she'd had sex. Harker could get as mad as he wanted. She was meeting Randy for dinner tonight.

She glanced at her watch. It was six o'clock. She'd been here since six that morning. She was done. She closed her laptop and slid it into the bag.

"I'd reconsider if I were you."

She jumped at Harker's deep, raspy voice. The man sounded like he'd swallowed sandpaper. She hated that his voice made her think of cool sheets and hot naked bodies. She pushed the image aside and stood. She'd step in front of a bus before she'd let him know how his voice affected her. "Well, you're not me." She slipped her laptop bag over her shoulder. "And I need time off. For the last ten months I've worked every holiday, weekend and late every night. I'm here almost as much as you are." That was saying a lot because his office was inside his home.

"You're really willing to give up this job, all this money for a date?" He leaned against the door frame. "This guy must be something pretty special."

"He is." She jutted out her chin. At least she hoped he was. She was tired of having no one in her life. During the day she was too busy to notice but at night, alone in her bed with her vibrator, it was pathetically obvious.

"How do you know? Didn't you say this was a first date?"

"Yes, but we've been talking for weeks now."

"When did you find the time? From what you claim, I've been working you every waking moment."

"I haven't been doing that on your time if that's what you're worried about. I can't believe you'd even think that." It hurt that he'd accuse her of cheating him. She worked her ass off for this man. "I thought you knew me better than that. I thought we were friends."

"Friends?" He smiled his lopsided smile that made him look like a mischievous boy. "Hardly. We've never been friends."

"Oh." That hurt more than she'd ever admit. This had happened to her all her life. People pretended to like her, so she'd help them with a project or their grades. She'd thought it'd end when she'd finished school, but work had been about the same. She was always the one people came to for help but never the one they invited to go out for lunch or drinks. She'd thought it was different here with Harker. The second day working here she'd forgotten her lunch and had realized that Harker hadn't eaten either. She'd ordered a pizza and had taken it to his office. They'd eaten lunch together almost every day after that and more dinners than she could count. But apparently, he was no different than everyone else. "Silly me. I have no idea why I thought that."

"Me either."

Oh, he was worse than the others. He wasn't even ashamed of using her. "Oh, we're being honest?"

"Of course."

"Then let me tell you why I thought you were my friend. We eat lunch and dinner together almost every day."

"We do."

"You got me tickets to the hottest night club around for New Year's Eve."

"A bonus for working Christmas Eve."

"You insisted on going with me."

"I had business to attend." He stepped into the office. "Plus, I assumed you'd need someone to look out for you and I was right."

"I'm a big girl. I can take care of myself."

"You could barely walk by the end of the night."

"I was having fun."

"Oh. Right. That car ride home was a great time. You drunkenly mumbling about all your failed relationships and"—his dark eyes seemed to almost glow—"your lack of recent sexual activity."

"I apologized for that." Her face still warmed. The fact that she hadn't had sex in months was embarrassing enough but telling him had been the worst thing she'd ever done when drunk and that was saying something. "I never would've opened up to you if I'd realized you were using me."

"Using is an interesting term."

"What do you mean by that?"

"Come to my office and we can talk." He moved aside to allow her to proceed him.

She took one step and stopped. She hated that her body obeyed this man without hesitation. "I can't. I have a date."

"Cancel it."

"No."

"Alison." He shook his head. "Don't push me on this. You won't be happy with the outcome."

"Don't push *me*, Gus." She didn't do well with ultimatums.

"Do not call me that." His jaw tightened.

She tried to stop herself, but her lips lifted in a smirk.

"I will fire you."

"Then do it because I'm going on this date." She pushed past him. He wouldn't really fire her. He needed her to meet his deadlines. Sure, he could find other application developers, but it'd take time for them to come up to speed and that'd put him way behind schedule. No, she was making her stand against his tyranny tonight. Life was too short. If he did fire her, she'd find another job. She'd done it before; she'd do it again.

CHAPTER 6: Harker

Harker followed Alison down the hallway, stopping at the entrance to the private section of his house. Her steps faltered as if nervous about continuing toward the door to the employee garage. She didn't need to worry because he wasn't going to let her get far.

"What time is your date?"

"Why?" She turned toward him.

"Because I'd recommend that you listen to my offer before leaving. I assure you that it'll be much more lucrative than any date."

"Offer? What are you talking about?"

It was time to gamble but he never risked anything without information. He opened the door and strode down the hallway and into the living room of his private quarters. He walked to the liquor cabinet and poured them each a drink. He hadn't even finished her gin and tonic before he heard her soft footsteps gliding across the carpet.

"I hate it when you don't answer me," she said.

"I know." He picked up the drinks and motioned to the sofa.

"I don't have much time, so you'd better hurry." She put her laptop bag on the couch next to her.

"You have plenty of time." He handed her the glass and tried not to look smug when she took it. "You just don't realize it yet." He sat on the chair across from her.

"This time you're wrong. I'm not working tonight. I haven't been on a date since—"

"Yes, I'm quite aware of how long it's been since you've dated." It made him harder than a stone, thinking of how long it'd been for her. Would she come at his slightest touch or would he have to reteach her the path to orgasm?

"How do you—"

"New Year's Eve, remember?"

"Oh. Right." She took a sip of her gin and tonic, her face heating slightly. "Then you understand why I'm so serious about this. And I'm done working ninety plus hour weeks."

"I pay you well for your time and you need the money."

"I do but not that badly."

"Are all the issues at your mother's house fixed already? Plumbing. Electric. Termites."

"I really wish I'd never thought of you as a friend."

"I'm glad you did." He smiled. "It made things easier."

"Things? Like what? Blackmailing me to work long hours because you know how bad my financial situation is."

"Your financial situation is fine but for some reason you've taken on your mother's problems." He didn't understand that, but it fascinated him. He had no obligations to anyone. Growing up unwanted and unloved made life so much easier.

"Because she's my mom." She said that like it made sense.

"Many wouldn't care."

"Many people are assholes." Her brow raised. "Present company not excluded."

"I'm a businessman. I make no apologies for that."

"Most businessmen are human first."

"I'm exceptional."

"Yeah, an exceptional jerk."

"Yet, you considered me your friend. Are you always friends with jerks?" He grinned. He loved winning these little arguments. He loved winning period but especially against a worthy opponent.

"I'm..." Her mouth opened and then shut, her lips turning downward in a frown. "Either tell me your offer or I'm leaving." She glanced at her phone. "I have to go home, shower, do my hair, makeup, find an outfit and it has to be the right one. Randy and I have video chatted, but this will be the first time we see each other in person, and I need to look—"

He had to shut her up. If she didn't stop talking about Randy and getting laid, he'd lean over and kiss her. Once his mouth touched hers there'd be no stopping him from tearing her clothes off and fucking her. It was time to dangle the bait and when she took it there'd be no wriggling loose. "I want to offer you co-ownership of Angel Face."

She stopped in mid-sentence, her mouth hanging open for one second and Harker's dick hardened. He wasn't a small man, but that wide mouth could swallow him whole.

CHAPTER 7: Alison

"What did you say?" Alison couldn't have heard Harker correctly. He wouldn't just give her co-ownership of Angel Face.

"You heard me." He took a sip of his drink. "I want to offer you partial ownership of Angel Face."

"I'd be part owner of my program?" Her heart raced. Angel Face was her baby, her creation. She'd never even dreamed this would happen. She'd just been happy being able to create something that might save women from being abducted and raped.

"Yes. You've done an excellent job and I believe in rewarding excellence."

"You do?" She had done an excellent job, but a tingle of suspicion danced in her head. Harker didn't praise; he barked orders and expected results.

"Yes." He sipped his drink. He wore his usual uniform—a white business shirt, and black slacks that matched his short, dark hair. He looked exactly like the rich urban businessman that he was. "I never praise anyone for a job well done. That's what I hire them to do and if they don't, I fire them. But you"—his dark eyes roamed up and down her body, making her insides tingle and sending that little suspicion in her head to a full-blown alarm—"have done much more than a good job and that calls for exceptional rewards."

"It does?" For one second, she was speechless but that didn't last. She could talk while puking. She'd done it many times in college. "Thank you. I didn't think you noticed or cared or...I'm just so happy." She smiled. "I always work hard, and Angel is such a great application. What we're doing...It's wonderful and I dreamt about being a bigger part, but I never thought—"

"Then you accept my offer?"

She grinned and started to speak but his words slipped past her happiness to her actual brain. "Offer? What's the catch?"

He smiled. It was slow and for some odd reason made her stomach flip and her pussy throb. Oh lord help her. If Gus Harker was turning her on, she really, really needed to get laid, but it wouldn't happen tonight. She glanced at her phone.

"Forget about your date."

"I can't."

"You can."

"I have to text Randy and let him know I can't make it."

"Go ahead. Text him." He flipped his wrist in a dismissive manner. "But then put the phone down."

"Fine." For co-ownership she'd stay and work tonight but she'd find a way to meet Randy tomorrow. She sent the text and slid her phone into her laptop bag. "Now, what's the catch," she repeated.

"I wouldn't call it a catch." He frowned.

"Of course, you wouldn't. You'd make up some business term or—"

"I do not make up business terms. I use them."

"Same difference."

His frown deepened, making creases in his cheeks where his dimples peeked out when he smiled. "It is far from the same thing."

"Says you. You twist things around to fit your plan."

"Everyone does that."

"Not me. I accept reality how it is. I don't try and change it." She'd learned in her pre-teens that wishing for something didn't make it happen. If it had, she'd have blonde hair and a perfect body. Some things weren't changeable and the things that were took a lot of work. She wiggled slightly. She should've been working on making her ass smaller instead of sitting in an office chair all day.

"You don't accept reality how it is."

"I do too." That was offensive. She took pride in that quality.

"You change everything the second you walk into a room or open your mouth."

"I don't talk that much." She knew she rambled. It annoyed almost everyone, but she couldn't keep the words inside her mouth. Her mother joked that her daughter didn't have a first word; she'd had a first soliloquy.

"Not that much?" He clamped his mouth shut and Alison was pretty sure she heard his teeth clank together at the force.

She should shut up. She shouldn't say a word. She should wait for him to speak but the words slipped out like always. "So, what's the catch. There has to be one. I can't believe you'd give me co-ownership because I did good...no excellent work. With you there has to be more than just a reward." She cringed as his eyes narrowed and his hand tightened around his drink. "Ah...you might want to be careful. I've never seen a glass shatter in someone's hand, but I think that'd hurt. All those shards of glass and—"

He put his drink on the table next to him before leaning forward and covering her mouth with one of his large hands. The other grabbed the back of her neck, keeping her in place. "There is no catch but there is more to the offer."

"Like what?" she mumbled against his hand as she pulled at his wrist.

He frowned again but let go of her and leaned back against his seat.

"I already work so much that I practically live here. I do want to be co-owner and I appreciate your offer, but I need some time off. I need a life. I'm done being your slave."

CHAPTER 8: Harker

"You're not my slave." But the idea intrigued Harker. Alison at his beck and call, doing everything he told her to do, submitting to his every command, eager to please him in any way he wanted. He'd make it good for her. His subs only complained when he left them.

"I may as well be."

"You have no idea how far you are from that position."

"Please." She rolled her eyes. "I'm here all the time. I do whatever you want."

"Not whatever I want." If she did, she'd be on her knees with his dick in her mouth.

"Name one thing that you wanted me to do that I didn't." She gave him a superior look.

He had to bite his tongue. Answering that question would be like tossing a rock in the water when the fish was nibbling on his bait. "We can talk about that later. Right now, we should discuss the details of your co-ownership."

"Oh. Yeah. Right." She smiled, a bit sheepishly. "I got sidetracked."

"You always do." It kept him awake at night wondering if she also got sidetracked in bed. He was mission oriented, but she'd be all over the place—first one spot and then another. It'd be unpredictable and exciting.

"Not always." She made a face at him and he almost smiled. She was the only one who ever made him smile from joy, not triumph. "But yeah, please tell me the details. I'm warning you though, I'm done working all hours seven days a week."

"Even for five percent ownership?" Merri and Tobias each owned fifteen percent, so that'd leave him sixty-five percent. Well over the fifty-one percent needed for control.

"Five percent?" She seemed less than thrilled.

"It'll be worth millions, maybe hundreds of millions."

"Oh." Her eyes grew distant.

He'd give her a few minutes to spend that money in her dreams, make her want it, see it. Let her envision what a life with that kind of money could mean. Then he'd reel her in. "Imagine what you could do with that money? You could start your own business."

"I could buy my mom a new house or fix that one." Her eyes almost glowed. "We could tear it down if she wanted and start from scratch."

"You could. Numerous times."

"I could buy a place nearby for Aunt Tiff too."

"Yes." He was astounded by her generosity. Most people thought of what they could do for themselves, but not her. He'd chosen well and it was time to feed her dreams. "You could start that program that you've talked about—the one to teach impoverished children how to use computers."

"I could give even the poorest kids access to computers." She smiled. "I could do so much."

"Yes, and the money will keep coming in. The software will have to be updated and maintained. We'll make it more marketable. We'll improve it and enhance it."

"Like a living thing." She smiled softly. "Sometimes I feel like it's my baby."

"Funny you should say that."

"Why?" She focused on him for the first time since he'd said millions. "I created Angel Face. I know it's not a real person, but it is part of me."

"Because that's what I want to discuss with you."

Her nose wrinkled, she did this when she puzzled something out and he found it adorable. "I don't understand."

"The other part of the deal. The part that you must agree to if you want co-ownership."

"The other part?" Her nose wrinkled more and then the confusion on her face cleared. "Oh, the catch."

"I wouldn't—"

"Just tell me. What is it? What do you want me to do now? I'm not working more. I can't. I don't think it's physically possible to work more than you already make me work."

"I agree." He had to force himself not to lean toward her and pounce on his prey.

"You do? To which part?"

"You work too much and that also stops with this deal."

"Really?" Her eyes widened in surprise.

"Yes. Once you agree and we sign the contract, I don't want you working more than sixty hours per week."

"Sixty?"

"I don't think we can cut back to forty, at least not until we staff up. I'm thinking another senior programmer, maybe two, and a few more at a junior level."

"You want to replace me?"

"No. I want you to be the lead. Train them. Let them take over the more tedious tasks."

"Oh." Her eyes got that distant glow again. "I'd be a good..." Her gaze sharpened as they met his. "I'd be their boss, right? Because I'm not going to spend time training people to have you work them until they quit or yell at them until they leave."

"I don't yell."

"Your nickname is Barker."

"My nickname? No one calls me that." His eyes narrowed as she tried not to laugh. "You made that up, didn't you?" His hand itched to put her over his knee and paddle that backside of hers but that was off limits. He wasn't bringing any of his kink into their bed. She'd be the mother of his child, not his sub or his lover. Okay, she'd be his lover but only for procreation, nothing else.

"I didn't make it up. You bark at me all day long and it just kind of...happened."

"That's the same thing as making it up and don't call me that. Even behind my back."

"You won't know."

"I'll know."

"How will you know? I'm not stupid enough to say it in front of anyone who'd tell you."

"I'll know by the look on your face."

"Fine but I'll think it." One side of her mouth slid upward in a half-smile. "All the time."

"I don't believe you will." Not after he'd fucked her and made her come over and over. She'd be putty in his hands, his to mold and transform.

"Okay. You're right, Gus. You're always right."

"Don't call me that either."

"Right. Sorry. Gu...Harker." This time she smiled like she'd won.

He couldn't wait to show her that she'd never had a chance to win this game.

"So, will I be their boss? It's the only way I'm going to train someone."

"You can be their boss and you'll need to train them well enough to fill in for you fulltime for a few months."

"Fill in for me for a few months? Why? Will I be going on a trip or something? I've always wanted to go on a business trip. Most people think it's boring, but I've always thought—"

"It's not a business trip, but in about nine or ten months you'll need some time off."

"I don't see why." Her nose wrinkled again and then her eyes brightened. "Unless you're giving me a vacation?"

"It's not a vacation."

"Then why will I need time off."

"To give birth. I've chosen you to have my baby."

"Your baby?" Her eyes almost popped out of her head and then she laughed. "Oh my god, Harker. You got me with that one." She laughed harder. "For one second I thought you were serious. Oh, I can't wait to tell Ellie. Did she put you up to this? She told me on New Year's Eve that you were attracted to me. I told her no way. Barker...I mean Harker isn't attracted to anyone. All the man does is work and yell orders." She rambled on, laughing the entire time.

It wasn't that funny. Actually, it wasn't fucking funny at all. Why did she think it was funny? He was rich, attractive and they got along well. She was semi-attractive, intelligent and within her childbearing years. This was insulting and her insults kept coming.

"I told Ellie that as far as I knew you didn't even date." She sobered for a moment. "Not that I have lately either. Neither of us have had the time but you're the boss. You could date if you wanted to which means you must not want to. Ellie said that you were a man so of course you wanted sex...had sex with someone. She thinks men's libidos are stronger than women's, but I say that's only true until they reach a certain age. When they get old, they don't want sex as much as—"

Good god, he had to stop her before she insulted him more. "I wasn't joking. I want you to have my child."

CHAPTER 9: Alison

Alison stared at Harker, waiting for him to crack a smile or to do something to let her know that he was kidding.

He tossed back his drink and stood, walking to the bar and refilling it. "I don't see why you think this is a joke. I'm offering you millions of dollars to have my child." He glanced at her, his frown deeper than normal. "This is a business deal, and I never joke about business."

"Business?" She laughed again but it fell flat when he continued to stare at her without even a spark of humor in his eyes. "You have to be kidding. You're trying to buy my baby? Who does that now-a-days?"

"People buy babies all the time, but they call it adoption." He made another drink for her and walked back across the room, handing it to her. "But I'm not talking about buying *your* baby. I'm paying you to have mine."

She stared at the two drinks in her hands. She'd barely touched the first one, but maybe she should. She raised one glass to her mouth and took a gulp but then put it down. Now wasn't the time to drink. Later, when she was home and away from this crazy man she could drink–a lot.

"I'm sure this is a shock." He sat, all suave businessman again. "I know it was a shock to me when I first began seeing you as the potential mother of my child."

"Wow. Flattery will get you nowhere but maybe you should try because insulting me will get you even less." She knew she wasn't attractive, but he didn't need to say it.

"I meant no insult." His frown deepened.

"Then double points for you because you managed to do it anyway." She stood. She wasn't staying here for this.

"Are you truly willing to give up millions of dollars and co-ownership of Angel Face because of hurt feelings?"

"That's not why I'm leaving. I just don't sell human beings." She could really use that money, but it was a baby. Her baby. His baby. Gus Harker's baby. She couldn't even fathom it. Would it frown all the time? Yell at her. Mom! I want milk! Now! What's taking you so long? Make that milk faster! She had to dig her nails into her palms to keep from bursting out in hysterical laughter.

"Sit. Please. As I said, I'm sure this is a surprise."

"Yes, you did say that right before you insulted me."

"I did no such thing. I said I was surprised when I started thinking of you as a potential birth mother for my child. I don't know why you'd think that's insulting. You should be flattered."

"Flattered." She was almost speechless. Almost. "Because you want to rent out my uterus?"

"Because I find you extremely intelligent, caring and warm. I only possess the first item in that list." His jaw tightened. "I know my assets as well as my flaws and I want to give my offspring the best start that I can. I'm not a warm person but I am intelligent and driven. I think our genes would create an excellent child."

"Our genes? You act like that's all there is to this."

"It is."

Her mind screeched to a halt. "So we won't...Oh. I'm so sorry." She sat back down. "I was thinking..." She wasn't going to admit that she'd thought they'd actually have sex. He'd laugh and she'd been insulted enough for tonight. "You're right. This might work."

"Of course, I'm right." He stood. "Give me one minute." He walked down the hallway to his office and returned, carrying a large manilla envelope. He handed it to her. "You'll want to hire a lawyer to read through these before signing."

"You drew up a contract?" She shook her head. "Never mind. Of course, you did. It's smart. We need to work out when we'd each see the child and all the logistics."

"When *we'd* see the child?"

"Yeah. Which holidays you'd have the baby. Which ones I would. We could alternate years. Like I get Easter one year and you the next. Most of the people at my last job were divorced so I know a lot about joint custody issues. We need to get that all settled so the child doesn't suffer."

"There won't be joint custody. The baby will be mine."

"And mine. You need my eggs. Unless...Do you have someone else's eggs you want to use? Do you only want me to carry the baby?" For some stupid reason she was a bit sad about that. She'd never really wanted kids but for those few minutes she'd imagined holding her baby and now she kind of wanted it.

"No. I said that our genes would make an excellent child. I'll need your eggs for that."

"Oh, that's right. You did say that." Her nose wrinkled slightly. "Then the child would be mine too."

"Technically yes, but you'll get co-ownership of Angel Face and I'll get my child."

"Our child and I can't do that." She didn't think she could shake her head any harder. "I'm not selling my baby."

"Not even for mill—"

"Not for any amount." She stood. "Forget it, Harker. Find someone else." She started for the door. Her mother would never forgive her. She'd never forgive herself.

"Wait."

She stopped. Damn that man. He spoke and her body obeyed.

"Remember all the good you can do with that money. Your mom's house. A place for your aunt. Those kids who only need a little help to flourish. Think of all the lives you can make better."

"How would I explain to my baby why I abandoned him or her? For money? So, I could help other kids while leaving him or her alone with you."

"I'll be an excellent father."

"Will you? You said it yourself; you're cold."

"I said I wasn't warm. There's a difference."

"Not to a child and I won't do that to my baby."

"It's millions of dollars."

"I don't care." She hurried toward the door before he could stop her again, but he didn't say a word.

CHAPTER 10: Harker

Harker stared at the spreadsheet he'd compiled of potential mothers. He had no idea how he'd overlooked this. Sometimes he was so focused on a goal that he missed the details. No woman as warm and caring as Alison would abandon her child and he didn't want a woman who would.

He grabbed his jacket and went into the garage. This wasn't over. Alison was the perfect candidate to be the mother of his child. He hadn't planned on sharing custody, but he'd concede on this point. All business deals had negotiations.

He got into his car and headed for Alison's house. The more he thought about it the more he realized that it was better this way. He worked a lot. He didn't want his child growing up in the care of nannies. Sharing custody would mean his child was with his or her parents more than paid caregivers.

By the time he pulled into the driveway at Alison's mother's house he was almost ready to thank her for being so stubborn. Having the mother share custody would free some of his evenings for amorous pursuits without guilt for leaving his child. Every other week or weekend he could go to La Petite Mort Club and engage in all his fantasies. His life would be perfect. He parked the car and walked to the house, ringing the doorbell.

"May I help you?" A woman peeked through a small window at the top of the door. She was older, but not unattractive with brown, wavy hair like her daughter's.

"Hello, Ma'am. I'm Harker. Alison's boss. I need to speak with her."

The woman opened the door. "Hi, I'm Estelle, Alison's mother. Please come in." She stepped aside. "I've wanted to meet you for a long time. Alison talks a lot about her job. I don't understand most of it, but I can tell she loves working for you."

"She's a dream employee." He'd had many dreams about her. Hot, sexy, wet dreams.

"She certainly works hard." There was a hint of chastisement in her tone. "And long hours."

He stepped inside the house. It was tidy but poor—worn drapes and carpet that had once been nice but was now threadbare. Stains on the ceiling signaled a leak—roof or maybe a plumbing issue. Either one worked for him because it meant that Alison definitely needed his money. "She does. We have a lot of work to do." He glanced at his watch. "May I speak with her?"

"She's not here."

"What do you mean she isn't here?" Then why the fuck was he in the house?

"She left."

"I understand the concept of she's not here."

Estelle's face pinched a bit around her lips.

"I'm sorry." He'd been too brusque. He needed to charm this woman. He was already at two strikes–rude and working her daughter long hours. He couldn't afford another one. "It's just that I need to speak with her. I want to discuss an offer I made her earlier tonight." Time to add some pressure to his case. "Did she tell you? It's quite lucrative." She wouldn't have told her mother. From what she'd said, dear mom was a bit old fashioned when it came to premarital sex.

"No, she didn't. What kind of offer?"

"Perhaps I should let Alison tell you. It's very good news."

"Yes, that's probably best." Estelle didn't sound happy about it.

"I wonder why she didn't mention it," he said.

"She probably forgot."

"Hmm. It's possible but the offer of a partnership in my business isn't something that slips one's mind."

"A partnership?" Estelle's face brightened. "That's wonderful. She's worked so hard for you."

"Yes, she has, and she should be rewarded." Oh, he'd reward her all right with sex, lots of it.

"That's wonderful. Oh, where are my manners? Would you like some coffee or tea?"

"Thank you. Coffee would be wonderful." He followed her into the kitchen. "Do you expect Alison home shortly?"

"Please, sit." Estelle motioned to the table and began preparing the coffee.

"I really do need to speak with her." He pulled out a chair and sat.

"Have you called her or texted?"

"This is better discussed in person." He'd known Alison long enough to know that right now, she'd ignore his calls and texts. When Estelle looked at him, he added, "There are contracts to sign."

"Oh, of course." She smiled. "I'm sorry but I don't know when she'll be home. She's on a date."

"Bloody hell. I thought she cancelled that." He stood. That wasn't going to happen. She wasn't having sex tonight. She wasn't getting laid until she was in his bed with his dick inside her. He wasn't in the mood to wait another month or two to make sure some other man's sperm hadn't impregnated her.

"Excuse me, Mr. Harker. I don't appreciate that language."

"Sorry." He was glad he hadn't said fuck, or he'd never get her help. "But this is a time sensitive issue." Yeah, his dick needed some release. "I need to speak with her tonight."

"I'll tell her to text you when she gets home. You can come back then."

That wasn't going to work. "Is there any way you could tell me where she went?" He had no problem interrupting her date. "I won't bother her for long." No, he'd convince her to leave. If she was that interested in getting laid, he had no problem whatsoever in going back to his place and fucking.

"I wish I could, but I really don't know where she went."

"Dam…shoot." He cringed. He hadn't said shoot since before his mom had started using drugs and bringing home drug dealers. He'd been dropping the F-bomb since he was eight. "Could you perhaps call her and ask her to come home?"

"Why don't you call her?" She sat the coffee on the table.

He patted his pockets. "I forgot my cell phone." He gave her a sheepish look. "I never remember to grab the da…dang thing." He never forgot his cell phone and prayed it didn't decide to beep now.

"Hmm. I don't know. I don't think she'd answer if I called. She's been looking forward to this date for a long time. Maybe my sister knows." She headed into the living room and over to the stairs before hollering, "Tiff come down to the kitchen. Alison's boss is here, and he needs to speak with her. Do you know where she went on her date?"

"I'll be right there," yelled another woman.

Estelle walked back into the kitchen. She poured another cup of coffee and carried the two mugs to the table. "I hope she can help. She and Alison have always been close." She took a sip of her coffee. "A young woman can tell her aunt things that she won't tell her mother."

He had no idea how to respond to that, so he drank some of his coffee. "This is very good."

"Thank you."

A woman walked into the kitchen. She was about the same height and age as Estelle but that was where the resemblance ended. This woman looked nothing like her frumpy sister. Tiff was probably in her late fifties or early sixties, but her hair was dyed blond, and she was thin and dressed in stylish, sexy clothes that hugged her hips and accentuated her breasts.

"Mr. Harker, this is Tiff, my sister," said Estelle.

"Mr. Harker. That seems formal," said Tiff.

"Call me Harker." He stood, shaking her hand.

"Harker? No first name?" asked Tiff.

"I'm not a fan of it."

"That's right. Alison did mention that." Tiff laughed and it was a throaty sound that went straight to his nuts. By the sparkle in her eyes this woman knew exactly what she did to men.

"She's spoken of me?" He didn't even want to know what she'd said. Alison had a tendency to say whatever passed through her brilliant head and there had been plenty of times that she'd been more than pissed off at him.

"All the time," said both women and then they laughed.

"Let me assure you." He gave them a half-smile. "I'm not as bad as she said."

"Oh, I bet you're just as bad," said Tiff with a twinkle in her eyes.

"Tiff don't be rude," chided Estelle, missing the innuendo. "Do you know where Alison went on her date? Mr. Harker needs to speak with her about a business matter."

"Business?" The humor left Tiff's eyes. "Would it be the matter that you discussed with her today?"

"She told you about the promotion?" asked Estelle. "She didn't mention it to me."

"You were making dinner," said Tiff. "Or I'm sure she would've." She gave an almost imperceptible shake of her head.

He understood. Nothing about that conversation had been or should be revealed to Estelle. He tipped his head and the tension in Tiff's eyes eased a bit. Now, he had to figure out if Aunt Tiff was a practical woman or a romantic. If she was the first, she'd be an invaluable ally but if she were the latter, he'd better make sure she didn't get ahold of a knife, or he might find it sticking out of his chest or his groin.

CHAPTER 11: Alison

"Thank you. Thank you. Thank you." Alison's heart slowed to a normal pace as she turned the car down their street and didn't see any flashing lights, but something was wrong. Her aunt wasn't prone to theatrics. She pulled into the driveway. Aunt Tiff wouldn't have texted her to come right home unless it was very important.

Randy had understood but he probably thought she was crazy for rescheduling the date, changing her mind and meeting him for dinner, only to leave half-way through for a family emergency. She'd be lucky if he answered her texts again. She hurried into the house. "Mom. Aunt Tiff. What happened? Is everything okay?"

She stepped into the kitchen and stopped. Harker sat at the table chatting with her aunt. He was still dressed in his black business pants, white button-down shirt and he looked large, impeccable, and out of place in her mother's kitchen. "What are you doing here? And how did you get here? I didn't see your car."

"I thought"—his eyes darted to Aunt Tiff—"that it'd be best if I moved the car down the street."

"There's no emergency is there?" She looked at her Aunt Tiff. She'd been betrayed.

When she'd told her aunt about the unbelievably horrible offer from Harker, Aunt Tiff hadn't seen it in the same light. Her aunt had been married four times and each man had been richer than the last. She'd still have money except Aunt Tiff's last husband had been diagnosed with Alzheimer's and her aunt had spent every dime she'd had for his care. Aunt Tiff had seen Harker's offer as a blessing. Alison had thought she'd made it clear that she had no intention of selling her child for any price.

"Of course, there is," said Aunt Tiff. "Harker wants to speak with you about that business offer."

"That offer has been refused."

"That offer should be reconsidered." Aunt Tiff smiled but her voice had an edge to it that Alison recognized. "All deals require negotiations."

"Exactly." Harker, the bastard, stared at her with a smirk on his face as he stood. "But we should talk about the details in private."

"There's nothing to discuss. I told you that some things aren't worth any amount of money."

Aunt Tiff snorted and smiled at Harker. "This one is young at heart and sometimes, soft in the head."

"I am not. I can't believe you think..." She glanced at her mother. At least she and Aunt Tiff agreed that this should not, could not be shared with her mother. "Harker, we have nothing further to discuss on this matter." She stepped away from the kitchen door. "You should go."

"Alison." Her mother's tone was like a slap. "This is my house, and you'll treat my guests with respect."

"Yes, mother." Alison literally bit her tongue to keep from saying—Yeah, your house that's falling down and wouldn't be livable if it hadn't been for her money fixing the plumbing and the electric.

"I'll have to remember that tone." Harker walked past her. He must've realized how hard it was for her to stay quiet because his half-smirk lifted, making him look like an evil clown. "I can never get her to obey me that easily."

"And you never will."

"We'll see about that." His confident grin sent a chill down her spine.

"I don't think we will." She'd just been challenged by the devil, but she wasn't backing down now.

"You should come with me." He motioned for her to proceed him out of the kitchen. "I'm ready to concede your point." His eyes locked with hers. "Like your aunt said, all deals require negotiations. I'll meet your demands. We should go to my"—he glanced at her mother—"office so you can look over the rest of the contract."

"No." Her stomach dropped to her toes. If he agreed to joint custody, she wasn't sure she could turn his offer down. Not only was it a lot of money but she'd be co-owner of Angel Face. She'd put her life into that software.

"Are you sure?" His gaze lifted above her head to the corner.

She knew exactly what he was looking at. The roof had leaked and the plaster on the ceiling was starting to crumble. This whole blasted place was falling down around them.

"This deal could help a lot of people." He glanced at her mother.

"I think you should at least hear him out," said Mom. "He agreed to your demands, whatever they were." Her mom hugged her and whispered, "I think you'll do an excellent job running a team of your own."

"He told you—"

"I explained that you'd be co-owner and run a team instead of working long hours doing everything yourself."

Of course, he'd only told her mom the parts that made him look good. It was typical Harker, but she was glad. Her mother would never understand the rest. Having a baby with a man Alison didn't love for money and career advancement was as foreign to her mother as an alien planet.

"Go with the man and hear what he has to say," said Mom. "You can always refuse again."

"It's not an ideal offer but I'm sure you'll get worse ones in life," muttered Aunt Tiff.

"It's a great offer." Harker sent her a dirty look.

Aunt Tiff shrugged. "Not terrible but I've had better."

"Better than co-owner of a successful company?" asked Mom. "What offer did you have that was better than that?"

"Marriage." Aunt Tiff's gaze darted to Alison and then to Harker.

He frowned but Alison understood the message. Her mom didn't approve of divorce, but she'd accept it. Having a baby out of wedlock would shame her mother at church. Marriage was the only option Alison had if she agreed to this offer.

"Fine. I'll go." This was perfect. Harker would never agree to marriage. His face had paled at the mere mention of the word. She grinned at Aunt Tiff. This decision would soon be out of her hands. "You're right. You have had better offers." She glanced at Harker and almost burst out laughing when his frown deepened, displaying his dimples.

"And Alison, be polite," said Mom.

"Oh, I'll be polite. I'll be super-duper sweet." She couldn't wait to see the panic in his eyes when she insisted on marriage. Then all she had to do was convince him that even though she wasn't the right woman to have his baby, she was the perfect woman to run the software engineering team.

CHAPTER 12: Harker

Harker waited at the door to his house for Alison. "I still don't know why you drove."

"Because this won't take long, and I didn't see any reason for you to have to drive me all the way back home."

"Stop being obstinate." The muscle in his cheek ticked from clenching his jaw so much. She was the most stubborn woman he knew. He opened the door and followed her inside.

"I'm not. I'm being practical. I've already given you my answer."

"I don't think you understand." He stopped at the bar in his living room and made each of them a drink. "I considered what you said about custody and I agree to your demands." He handed her a glass.

"What you're actually saying is that I was right, and you were wrong." The smug look on her face made his hand itch to paddle her backside.

"No, I'm saying that there was merit to your suggestion." He sat on the chair next to her.

"Merit to wanting to take care of my own kid." She half snorted. "No kidding but why do you want a kid? Why don't you already have them? At your age—"

"I'm not that much older than you are." He was getting a little tired of her referring to him as old.

"How old are you?" She studied him. "Forty...five, forty-six? That'd make you fourteen or fifteen years older than me."

"I'm forty." He leaned closer to her. "Which means that if I don't want to be ancient when my child graduates from high school, I had better start now." The blood rushed to his dick at the thought. He couldn't wait to get all her energy in his bed and focused on him.

"That's true." She wrinkled her nose in thought. "You should. You have to figure at least a year from the time you start trying to when she should deliver."

He didn't like her referring to the mother as she instead of I, but he'd ignore it. "Exactly." He handed her the papers that he'd given to her earlier. "Read through this and let me know if you have any questions. Then, I'd suggest you take it to your lawyer." He handed her a business card. "Tell him or her to contact my lawyer if they have any questions."

"Oh, I don't need any of this." She handed the contract and the business card back to him. "You'd better start looking for another woman because I'm not having your baby."

"Why the fu…" He cleared his throat, getting his temper in check. "I thought your only objection was custody." He'd spent months choosing her; he wasn't letting her go.

"It was." She sipped her drink, trying unsuccessfully to hide her smug expression.

"Then I don't understand the issue." He leaned toward her. "Remember. I'm a businessman. I'm willing to negotiate." His eyes skimmed down her body. Damn he couldn't wait to strip her bare. Her breasts were small and her hips wide. She didn't have the perfect body, but he was dying to spend hours exploring every inch.

"I don't think you're this willing."

He raised his gaze, expecting to see her cheeks flushed from his blatant perusal of her body but she just stared at him with a polite expression on her face. The muscle in his cheek ticked faster. Women did not look at him like he was a eunuch. "Are you willing to give up all that money and all those wonderful things you can do with it?"

"I was thinking about that. Even though I'm not the right woman to have your kid doesn't mean that I'm not the right person to head up the software engineering department. We need a team if we're going to—"

"We are not taking the child out of this deal."

"You said you were a businessman. I want to negotiate."

"And I will but not about the child."

"You can still have the kid, just not with me and I can run the software part of your business."

"No."

"I understand that you won't want to give me five percent. How about three percent and I run your team? That's one worry off your plate. You can spend more time looking for the perfect mother for your child."

"No." He leaned back because if he didn't, he'd probably strangle her or kiss her to shut her up. "Listen very carefully. I'm willing to negotiate but there is no deal—none—without you agreeing to have my child." He wanted to fuck her, to see her round with his baby and he always got what he wanted.

"The problem is, Gus"—she stressed his name and the tick in his cheek almost did the cha-cha—"that I don't think you're willing to agree with what I need in order to have your child."

"Name it." Right now, he'd agree to almost anything to be able to rip her shirt off and discover the color of her nipples. His bet was peach because of her coloring but they could be a dusky rose or even brown.

"My mother is very religious."

"I'm aware of that." He had a hard time raising his gaze away from her chest. She wore a black silky shirt that made him wonder about her bra and panties. Had she put on sexy lingerie for her date? Would her hard little nipples push through the lace, begging for his lips? He cleared his throat. "She's a lovely woman." He smiled slightly as he lifted his eyes away from her breasts. "Not overly fond of cursing."

"You have no idea. Even the smallest thing sets her off and she's way more accepting of you cussing because you're a man. It's one of those things that men do."

"I am that, and I'm glad you finally recognize it." He was a virile male, not some old limp-dicked geezer.

"I know you're a man." She laughed. "I mean not a man's man, but you are a male."

"What do you mean by that." He leaned forward and put his hand over her mouth, stopping her from speaking. "No. Don't answer that." He wasn't sure his ego could take it. "Just tell me what you need in order to sign those papers." He dropped his hand and tapped the contract.

"I need you to marry me," she said.

"Ma..." His throat closed up and he choked on the word.

CHAPTER 13: Alison

"Having a child out of wedlock would kill my mother." Alison did her best not to burst out laughing at the look on Harker's face. Obviously, the baby bargain was off. Now all she had to do was convince him to go forward with the rest of it...or most of the rest of it.

He cleared his throat. "Marry?"

"Yeah. I thought about your offer. I really did and I could use the money, but I can't do that to my mother."

"People who aren't married have kids all the time."

"And my mom prays for them." She rolled her eyes. "You should hear her. She talks about them in hushed tones, saying how embarrassing it must be for their poor parents." She leaned forward, resting her hand on his knee. "She even says things like, thank God Alison isn't like that. Then she goes on to say that even though I may never marry—she can't help getting that dig in—at least I won't humiliate her and my dead father."

His eyes grew dark as he stared at her hand on his leg. He was going to bolt soon. She needed to hurry and make her pitch. She wanted to be co-owner and she was going to do her best to get it.

"So you understand that I can't have your child but that doesn't mean we can't move forward with the rest of the deal. I deserve to be co-owner and you need more than just me for the work we have now and all the future enhancements to the software. I'd be a great boss. I'm fair and kind. You know I work hard. Merri is always talking about how dedicated I am and—"

"How does she feel about divorce?"

"Who? Merri?"

"Your mother." He raised his eyes to hers, and his were as black as a night with no stars.

Her instincts sensed something almost primal in his gaze and she leaned away from him, folding her hands on her lap. The one that'd been touching his knee seemed to be warmer than the other as if his heat had branded her. "She...she's grown used to it. She doesn't like it, but she can't really take a stand on that one because almost everyone she knows has a kid who's been divorced at least once."

"Then I agree. We'll get married." He handed her the papers. "Look these over. The wedding with be soon." His eyes almost glowed as they raked across her body. "Very soon."

CHAPTER 14: Harker

"You want to marry me?" Alison looked like she'd just been pushed from an airplane.

"No, but I'll do it." Harker had to admit it made him happy to surprise her. She'd thought she had him neatly trapped, but he wasn't a novice at negotiations. If he wanted something, he'd do whatever it took to get it, and he wanted her.

"Oh. Wow. You..." Her mouth opened and shut but nothing else came out.

He wanted to laugh. This was the first time he'd ever seen her speechless. It wouldn't last long but he'd enjoy it while he could.

"You will?" Her face paled.

"Yes." He leaned forward, inhaling her scent. She always smelled fresh and slightly floral. He hadn't figured out if it were a perfume or body lotion but whatever it was it made him horny as hell. "You should think of what day we're going to be married because if you don't decide, I will and that means it'll be tonight."

"Tonight?" She almost jumped from her chair.

"Yes." His gaze dropped to her chest again. He was hard and ready for his wedding night. "We could fly to Vegas and be home by Monday for work."

"Oh, we can't tonight. We can't at all." Her face was pale now and her intelligent eyes were panicked, scrambling to find a reason why they couldn't get married.

"Why not?" It was time to push her into that corner and win this game. "I agreed to your terms."

"We can't just get married. That's crazy." She leaned as far away from him as she could without getting up and leaving the room.

"Why is it crazy? We've known each other for a year. We're both single, available, and we both want what the other is offering."

"But...that's so cold."

"Marriages have been business arrangements for longer than they've been love matches and the ones that are business arrangements are happier and more successful."

"You're suggesting that we stay married?" The horrified look on her face was beyond insulting.

However, if he were honest the idea of being married to her or anyone for the rest of his life made him want to run in the other direction. He'd never even considered marriage. He went to the Club for sex when he was in the mood. He even formed relationships there when he wanted. They were simple and uncomplicated, based on mutual desire. He had work and a select few friends. He had everything he wanted except a child. "No. I'm suggesting that we marry and once you deliver a live child—"

"I can't believe you said that." She clutched her stomach as if she were already protecting a baby.

"I'm not handing over part of my company for a miscarriage."

"Of course not but you shouldn't talk about it."

"Why?"

"I'm sure it's bad luck or something."

"I wasn't aware you were superstitious."

"I'm not but...don't say that again."

"Okay, but it's in the contract."

"That's fine. It should be but we don't need to talk about it."

"Fine with me." The less they discussed the contract the better. "After you deliver a"—he paused for a second—"child, you'll get five percent co-ownership of Angel Face and the right to hire your own software team. I'll have the final approval on all new hires. Then we'll divorce, keeping joint custody of the baby. I'll need my lawyer to add in the part about the marriage and divorce, but the rest of the contract will be the same." It was an attractive offer. He was being more than generous.

Her lips pursed. "You don't get the final say on who I hire for my team."

"I'm afraid I can't let you just hire anyone. There are security matters—"

"I'll make sure that they meet those, but I have to be the boss."

"This is a business. I can't let your inexperience affect my bottom line."

"I choose who I want to hire and between the four of us we decide." She frowned.

"The four of us?"

"You, me, Tobias and Merri. We're all co-owners so we should all have a say in the new hires for the business."

Right now, he didn't care about anything but dragging her to his bedroom and fucking her until neither of them could move, but this was his business. "I make all the final decisions on employees. I do this for Merri's staff and Tobias's as well."

"You do? I thought Merri hired everyone."

"She chooses the candidates, but I make the final decision. I usually agree with her choices."

"Oh. I guess that's okay then."

His mouth dried like he'd eaten a bag of cotton. This was it. He was getting married. His throat tightened and his stomach twisted. He took a sip of his drink. It was a business arrangement, nothing more but for some reason it felt like a lot more.

CHAPTER 15: Alison

"Look it over and let me know if you or your lawyer have any questions. I'll give you a copy of the marriage addendum tomorrow." Harker handed Alison the contract.

"Tomorrow? It's Saturday." This was all moving too fast.

"My lawyer works whenever I need him to."

"Why am I not surprised." She flipped to the first page. "I can't believe I'm actually doing this," she muttered as she began reading the document. "I'm not changing my name." She looked up at him. "What name should we give the baby?"

"I suggest we discover if it's a boy or a girl first."

"No." She laughed. "I mean the last name. I'm not changing my name—"

"The child will have my last name. That's not negotiable."

"Oh." This man was so bossy and arrogant, but she loved knocking him down a peg. "Then I get to pick the first name."

"Fine."

"If it's a boy—"

"You are not naming him Gus. I'm serious about that."

"You agreed. It's my choice." She grinned.

"It is, but not that name."

"Why do you hate your name so much?" She'd never met anyone who had such an aversion to their name. "Gus is a nice name. Strong. A little old fashioned but it fits you."

"I'm not old," he said through gritted teeth.

"I know. I just meant that it fits with your generation."

He inhaled deeply. "That's the same as calling me old."

Alison was quite aware that he was trying to control his temper. People had been doing that around her all her life.

"Please, focus and read the contract. I want this child born before I turn fifty."

She began to read the document again, but hundreds of questions ran through her head and that meant out of her mouth. "When will I have to see the doctor? I'll need to know so I can set a date for the wedding. My mom is going to want a big affair, but I'll convince her that small is better. Only immediate family and a few friends. I don't want anything big because this isn't real. I'll save all the special things for my next marriage." She paused. "My next marriage. I never thought I'd say something like that. I'd always thought that I'd be like my mom and marry once but I guess—"

"We can get the bloodwork done tomorrow. I'll set up the appointment. We can be married on Sunday."

"Sunday? This Sunday? As in two days from now?" Her throat almost closed with panic. This was all happening so quickly.

"Yes, why wait? I told you I want this child to graduate before I'm sixty."

"I know that, but did you set up the appointment with the clinic? I'd imagine that'd take some time. I'm sure they have to run tests and it doesn't always take the first time."

"What clinic? The bloodwork shouldn't—"

"The in vitro fertilization clinic."

He stared at her like she was talking out of her nose.

"You know, so I can get pregnant. Have your baby."

"We aren't going to a clinic."

"We aren't?"

"No."

"Then where? Oh, a hospital. I don't know why I thought it was done at a clinic." She knew almost nothing about in vitro fertilization, but she'd be reading up on it tonight.

"We won't be going to a hospital either, at least not until you're ready to deliver."

"Then where will we go to get me pregnant?"

"Here."

"Here? I've never heard of at home in vitro fertilization."

"We won't be using in vitro fertilization." He seemed amused.

"Then I don't understand. Is there a new way to put your sperm with my egg? In vitro is the only method I've heard of. I haven't done any research on it but—"

"It's not new. Not at all."

She stared at him, confused.

"We'll be doing it the old-fashioned way. I know you've heard of that." His lips twitched like he was fighting not to laugh. "I've heard you complain about your lack of that on several occasions."

"You mean sex?" She blinked. He had to be joking.

"Of course, I mean sex."

"I can't have sex with you." She dropped the contract on the table.

CHAPTER 16: Harker

Harker was no longer amused. "And why can't you have sex with me?"

"Because...because you're Gus. Barker. You're...well..." Alison waved her hand at him. "You're you."

"What is wrong with me?" He'd never, ever been treated like this. "I'm a man and I can assure you that although I'm older than you everything works. Exceptionally well."

"Oh...no. Oh, god. I didn't mean to insult you."

"I don't know how it could be taken any other way."

"I'm sure you're great...fabulous in bed and everything but, it's just that..."

His pride should be eased a bit, but he knew Alison too well. The fatal attack was coming. He had to shut her up before it arrived, or he might have to find someone else to have his child. He leaned forward and clamped his hand over her mouth. His other hand tangled in her hair, holding her still. "Do not say another word." Her eyes widened, staring into his. "I want you to think. *Really* think of what you can and will do for millions maybe billions of dollars. Do you understand?"

She nodded.

"Are you sure? If you go too far and say too much the deal is over. So, think long and hard about what you're about to say. I know that concept is foreign to you and"—he felt a little better when her eyes narrowed—"you can't help it that your thoughts spill from your mouth like vomit." Now her eyes were hurt. He almost felt bad but damn it, she'd butchered his pride numerous times today. She deserved a little payback. "I'm going to let go of you now." He tightened his hold on her hair for one second. "Think before you speak and if you can't do that then don't speak." He slowly lifted his hand from her face and shifted away from her.

She straightened, opened her mouth. Closed it. Opened it again and took a deep breath. "Why can't we do in vitro? I've heard..." She closed her mouth quickly.

Because I'm dying to fuck you probably wasn't the right answer since she so obviously didn't return the sentiment. "In vitro is for couples who have issues conceiving. I'm not taking it off the table, but I believe we should try the natural method first."

She wrinkled her nose. He wanted to shout, *come on*. He was a catch. He was rich, successful, in shape and women found him very attractive. He even had several regular arrangements with women at La Petite Mort Club and they weren't Pleasure Associates. They were rich, attractive, sensual women.

"I think we should try in vitro first," she said.

"No."

"Why not? It can't be the expense. You have more money than you can spend."

"First, I have more than I can spend because I don't like to waste it and going straight for in vitro is a waste of money."

"But I'd prefer—"

He'd better talk fast before she got rolling. "Second, female orgasms increase the likelihood of conception and I doubt you'll orgasm at the doctor's office."

"Really? I never heard that."

"It's theory but the science backs it."

"Oh." Again her nose wrinkled. "I guess we could try but if it doesn't work...How often do we have to do it before we opt for in vitro?"

"I think we need to suffer through it a few times. A month at least."

"A month? Is that once a day? Once a week?" She sounded so horrified that Harker wasn't sure his poor dick would ever stand up to play again.

"Perhaps you're right. This isn't going to work." He grabbed the contract.

"I'm sorry. You know I say whatever rolls through my head. I didn't mean to hurt your feelings." She touched his hand. "I am sorry. I just...I've never thought of you like that."

"Like what? A man?" Part of him was done with this but another part wanted to grab her hand and hold it. He'd been dreaming of touching her since she'd brought the pizza to his office for lunch.

He'd been fascinated by her energy and chatter from the first day he'd met her but the fact that she'd noticed he hadn't eaten lunch had twisted his insides. No one ever thought of his comfort unless he paid them to do so.

"No. I know you're a man, but I've never thought of you as a man I'd date...or have sex with. Not because of you but because you're my boss. I don't date men I work with. Ever. Especially my boss. As a woman in a man's field this is something that you can't do no matter what."

"I can understand that." It made sense and soothed his pride.

"I don't think you can, not really. You're a man. If you get a promotion or a raise no one whispers about who you slept with or what you had to do to earn it. Women have to keep everything completely professional all the time."

"Does this mean you're going to sign the contract?" He turned his hand so hers rested on his palm. It was the closest he'd get to holding her hand until she was his.

There were shadows in her eyes, but she nodded. "I guess it does."

CHAPTER 17: Alison

"Alison are you sure about this?" asked Ellie.

"No." Alison stared at herself in the mirror. She wore a white dress that hugged her hips with a scooped neckline to accentuate the little cleavage she had. Her hair was pulled up in a neat chignon with a few tendrils draping around her face. Her mother had insisted on a hat with a small veil, but she wasn't putting that on until she had to.

"Then don't do this." Ellie took her hand. "Marriage is forever."

"Where's my mom?"

"She went to get your hat and veil."

Alison glanced at the door to make sure her mom wasn't standing there. The woman had some superpower that allowed her to catch someone doing something they weren't supposed to be doing. As a kid Alison had wondered if her room had been bugged. Researching that had been her first foray into technology. "Not this marriage. It should only last about a year." Her stomach fluttered. "One year and I'll be co-owner of my own business, a very successful one, and Angel Face will be mine, or part mine."

"And you'll have a child"—Ellie squeezed her hand—"with a man you don't...What do you feel for Harker?"

"It doesn't matter what I feel for him." She pulled her hand away. Ellie was supposed to be on her side, but all her friend had done the entire week since Alison had told her about her pending marriage and the contract was to try and talk her out of it. "I've always wanted a child someday."

"And you'll have one with someone you love."

"Oh, please. I'm not lucky like you." She'd never admit it, but she'd always been a bit envious of her friend. Ellie had never spent more than a few days without a man in her life. Whereas Alison's experience had been the opposite.

"I wouldn't call myself lucky." Ellie's eyes brightened. "Until Adrian I had the worst luck."

"At least you had hope of getting married and having a family. I never had that. I had one eighteen-month relationship in college that ended when we graduated. After that, I've had nothing but short term...flings. A month or two but nothing that lasted long enough for me to even dream of a family." She swallowed. The truth was hard to accept but lying to herself was worse. "Harker is offering me that and financial security."

"But you don't love him."

"So. I'll love our baby." She'd finally have someone to pour all her love into and that child wouldn't care if she talked too much or said inappropriate things. It'd love her because she'd show it nothing but love from the day it was born.

"Oh honey, please don't do this. You'll find someone. Your perfect man is out there. You just need to stop working so much and—"

"Enough Ellie, I'm doing this." Her eyes teared up. "I want you to be on my side but if you can't it's fine." It wasn't at all. "Please don't try and talk me out of it."

"Of course, I'm on your side." Ellie hugged her. "I've always got your back." She smiled but it was forced. "If anyone can make this work it's you. You're the strongest most wonderful person I know."

"I have no intention of even trying to make this work. I don't know why you won't believe that. I'm going to marry him, get pregnant, have the baby and then we'll get an amicable divorce."

"I hope you're right, but I've lived with a lot of men and it's never that simple. You're a kind and loving person. You find a way to love and care for everyone you meet. If you truly don't mean for this to last then please, protect your heart."

"From Harker?" Alison laughed. "That's not a problem. I like the man. I respect him but I'll never fall for him." She wrinkled her nose. "I can't even imagine having sex with him."

"Why not? He's gorgeous."

"You think so?" She shrugged. "I did think he was attractive when I first saw him but now"—she made a face—"he's just grumpy Gus Barker to me."

"I can't believe you don't see how sexy he is." Ellie sighed. "With that domineering attitude and the gray at his temples. I swear if the man hadn't had the hots for you, I would've made a play for him on New Year's Eve."

"Instead of Adrian? Right." Ellie's boyfriend Adrian was the most attractive man Alison had ever seen outside of the movies.

"Okay, not once Adrian arrived but before then, yeah."

"Maybe we should ask Harker if you can be my surrogate." Alison grinned. "You can sleep with him."

"I don't think Adrian would agree to that, plus how would you two mingle your brilliant genes and create this super child?"

"Little details. We can work those out later." She laughed.

"I think those are more than little details but even if we could, I'd have to decline. You can have that sexy man all to yourself."

Alison grimaced. "I guess I'll just close my eyes and hope he's fast. I'm sure he will be. Most men only last a few minutes."

"Not in my experience and I have to warn you, Harker is alpha male all the way. I doubt sex is going to be quick"—Ellie's eyes softened—"but when a man knows what he's doing it's better than wonderful."

A knock sounded on the door. Ellie walked across the room.

"Oh, please. It's my wedding day. Let me have my dreams of quick sex and a fast pregnancy so I can get this all over..."

Ellie opened the door. "Harker. What are you doing here?" She glanced at Alison and stepped in the doorway, partially closing the door behind her. "You're not supposed to see the bride until your wedding day."

"It is my wedding day and her mother got lost. I was directing her to the room."

Alison wanted to run and hide. He had to have heard her, didn't he? She moved closer to the door to listen.

"Then where is Mrs. Robinson?" asked Ellie.

"Annie, the caterer, stopped to ask her a quick question. She's over there." He tipped his head to the right. "I thought I'd give Alison a heads-up. She's said many times how her mother has the worst timing. I didn't want her to overhear something about our wedding that she shouldn't."

Alison bit her lip, shifting closer. Harker didn't sound upset. Did that mean he hadn't heard her?

"That was nice of you," said Ellie. "Thank you."

"I'll see you both in the living room in a few minutes."

Ellie stepped into the room, closing the door and leaning against it.

"Do you think he heard me?" Alison started to pace. "I couldn't tell from his voice. Did he seem upset? Damn it. I didn't want to hurt his feelings. If he heard me, I'm going to have to apologize, and he doesn't make that easy."

"He may not have heard you. The doors are thick."

"But he has excellent hearing, and you opened that door while I was saying I wanted to get this over with."

"If he did hear you, say you meant the wedding. That's normal."

"Yeah. I guess, I can say that. You don't think he heard the sex and pregnancy bit?"

"No." Ellie shook her head, but Alison knew her friend well enough to see the lie in her eyes.

CHAPTER 18: Harker

"It's time," said Tobias.

Harker turned from the window, his stomach in knots. He'd spent every moment since he'd gone to the bedroom trying to figure out what he should do. He wasn't particularly excited to fuck a woman who couldn't wait to get it all over, including sex with him, but the contracts were signed, and he had a fortune and a business to leave to someone. He refused to give everything he'd worked for to charity and his mother's family wasn't getting a penny.

"It's not too late to change your mind," Tobias whispered. "I don't think anyone here, including the bride, would object."

"She certainly wouldn't as long as she got her partnership and her team." It came out harsher than he'd meant but it was the truth. Alison was even less thrilled about this marriage then he was. At least he'd been interested in creating the baby, but that was before she'd made it perfectly clear how she felt about him.

"Then don't do this. She deserves both. It won't be losing to give her those things."

"And I deserve nothing in return?"

"You deserve to be happy, and I don't think this is going to do that for you."

"I'll be happy when I have my child." He straightened his suit jacket. "Let's get this over with." He almost smiled. That was exactly what Alison had said.

"Harker, think about—"

"My mind is made up."

Tobias shook his head. "You're the most stubborn person I've ever met."

"That's a lie." He headed for the back of the room where the minister was waiting. "You know Merri."

"True." Tobias laughed. "But you take second place."

"I'll accept that." He stopped at the minister's side and Tobias stood by him as his best man.

"You have the ring?" asked the minister.

"Yes." Tobias patted his pocket.

"Good. Good. Let's begin."

The minister's wife, who sat at the piano, began playing the wedding march. Harker turned with the others to see his unwilling bride enter the room, except no one came. Sweat gathered under his collar. Getting stood up at the altar hadn't been on his list of things to do before he died.

"Maybe someone got a lick of common sense," whispered Tobias.

He didn't say anything. Alison had damn well better show. If she'd had second thoughts, the least she could've done was sent him a text. She didn't need to make him look like a fool in front of...

Ellie stepped from behind the doors, a beautiful smile on her pretty face. The constriction around Harker's chest eased as she walked down the aisle, but his gaze was focused behind her, searching for Alison.

He hadn't seen her in almost two days. He'd hoped to catch a glimpse of her when he'd gone to his bedroom, but Ellie has been quick to close the door and all he'd seen was a flash of white. He wouldn't admit it, but he missed Alison—the constant chatter, the way she rambled on spewing any thought that slipped into that brilliant mind of hers. He prayed his child got her brains. No other women on his list had been even close to her in intelligence and drive. Alison worked like her life depended on it. Those two factors were the reasons he'd chosen...All thoughts fled as she stepped into view.

She was beautiful. Her hair was pulled back, framing her pale face. He wanted to yank that hat off her head so he could see her better until his gaze traveled down her body. Fuck. He'd had no idea she had cleavage. Her creamy skin looked softer than silk and the simple white dress hugged her hips, making him want to bend her over his couch or a table—anything as long as her ass was in the air, teasing him, begging him to slap it. His mouth dried as every drop of liquid in his body rushed to his dick.

At least he no longer worried about embarrassing himself on his wedding night but if he didn't get his cock under control, he might embarrass himself during his wedding.

CHAPTER 19: Alison

Alison's feet moved as slowly as possible down the hallway that led from the bedroom to the living room. She was ready to puke. She couldn't believe she was going through with this.

"Hurry up," whispered Ellie. "Unless you're changing your mind."

"I'm not." Alison took another step.

"Then get moving." Ellie stood at the doorway to the living room. "Harker has to be nervous standing up there waiting for you."

"Too bad. He's the idiot who agreed to this. I never thought he would. Who agrees to marry someone just to have a kid?"

"You for one." Ellie motioned for her to hurry up. "So, either tell me to go out there and cancel this or get your ass over here."

"Go. I'll be there in a minute." She forced herself to move forward.

"Don't take too long." Ellie opened the door, propping it open behind her before walking into the living room.

Alison took another step and another. One year. That was it. Not even a year if she got knocked up tonight. Oh lord, please make Harker be as fertile as...well, she didn't know what was super-duper fertile. Damn it. They should've been tested. What if one of them couldn't have a kid? All this would be for nothing. She stopped. One more step and she'd be in the doorway. "That long hallway wasn't long enough," she muttered as she glanced behind her. She could run. No one had seen her yet, but she'd lose too much. She moved forward and stepped into Harker's living room.

The twenty or so guests were all facing in her direction. Her mom and aunt were smiling and wiping tears from their eyes. Her stomach felt like she'd eaten bad fish, but she kept putting one foot in front of the other as she prayed that she didn't actually puke. One year. That was it. The flowers shook in her hands and she kept her head bowed because she'd bolt if she looked at him.

She stopped when she saw his shoes—dark and so shiny that she could see her reflection. A strong hand grabbed her upper arm. She gasped at the warmth of his touch. He turned her toward him and then his hand was gone but only for a second. He touched her chin, raising her head before lifting her veil.

She kept her eyes down. *One year. Then it'd be over.*

His finger pressed against her lips and her eyes flew to his. Oh god, she'd mumbled that. His dark gaze was unfathomable, and it make her stomach twist even more.

"I'm sor—"

He captured her chin and bent, stopping when his lips were next to her ear. "Hush." He dropped his hand and straightened as he turned toward the minister.

She followed his lead.

"Dearly beloved," said the minister as he started the ceremony.

She bit her lip to keep from saying anything out loud but in her mind, she said one year. That was all. All? It sounded short but that was 52 weeks. 365 days. 8760 hours. The flowers shook so hard in her hands that the minster paused, his eyes on the bouquet.

Harker took her hand, prying the flowers from her grasp and slapping Tobias in the chest with them before pulling her close to his side. His warmth gave her strength. They could do this. They were kind of friends. He wasn't a bad guy. He just wasn't the man for her. Still, she'd taken jobs she didn't like. That was it. She'd consider this a job. She had to stay here a little over nine months and when she left, she'd be financially secure. She'd done way worse than that.

"I do." Harker's deep voice sent a fissure of fear or something into her belly.

Shit they were already at that part. She could do this.

"Alison," prompted the minister.

"Oh...oh, yeah. I do." Her face heated at the few chuckles from the crowd.

"The rings," said the minister.

Harker let go of her right hand and took her left. "With this ring, I thee wed, and with it, I bestow upon you all the treasures of my mind, heart, and hands."

Her hand trembled in his grasp and then Tobias handed her a ring. She took it and slid it onto Harker's finger.

"With this ring..." Her mind went blank. This had never happened to her. The words she'd memorized were gone. She stared up at him.

"I thee wed," he whispered.

"I...I thee wed."

"And with it," he continued softly.

"And with it," she repeated, waiting on the next part because her mind was still empty. Harker continued and she repeated his words. She had no idea what she said. She could've said she'd give him her right lung and her left breast for all she knew but after a few more phrases it was over. She almost collapsed from relief until she heard...

"You may now kiss your bride."

Harker was going to kiss her. Her stomach started to shimmy up her throat and everything slowed down. He lowered his face toward hers. She didn't mean to move but the next thing she knew she'd shifted away from him. His eyes darkened and his frown deepened, showing his dimples. Then everything sped up as if released from a spring. He captured her chin in his hand and the warmth of his touch on her cool skin made her shiver. His mouth lowered. She had to do this. She had to get it over with. She leaned forward as he bent, and her forehead slammed into his nose.

"Son of a bitch." His hand dropped from her chin and grabbed his face.

She stood on tiptoes and kissed the back of his hand before turning and smiling at the crowd. "We're married."

Everyone stared past her. Their faces filled with surprise. She glanced behind her. Harker's head was tipped back, and his once pristine white shirt was splattered with blood.

"Oh my." She should help him but instead she edged away.

"Oh, no." He reached out, grabbing her hand and stopping her from running down the aisle away from him.

CHAPTER 20: Harker

"I think it's time for us to go." Tobias finished his drink and stood.

"Already?" It was late but Harker wasn't eager to be alone with his bride. He'd spent the day chasing her down and holding her hand to stop her from running away from him. What he hadn't been able to do was to keep her from drinking. The last time he'd seen her, which was over two hours ago, she'd been well on her way to plastered. He'd never expected to marry but if he had this was the exact opposite of how he would've imagined his wedding day.

"Yes. We're the last ones here besides Adrian and Ellie. Even Alison's mom has gone home," said Tobias.

"Harker, take some time off." Merri stood from the chair next to her husband. "Go on a honeymoon. Get to know each other as people not boss and employee."

"It's Saturday. We have all day tomorrow."

"Wow. One day." Merri gave Tobias a disbelieving look.

"We discussed this, and you heard Alison say that we didn't need a honeymoon. We both prefer to work."

"What was she supposed to say when you explained how it wasn't a real marriage?" asked Merri. "The only answer she could give and not be humiliated was to agree with you."

"Humiliated? Why would she be humiliated?" If anyone was humiliated it was him. At least he wasn't counting the seconds until they could divorce.

"Ask her what she wants to do, Harker. Talk to her."

"No need. She made it clear." A woman who couldn't spend thirty minutes standing next to him in a crowd of her friends wouldn't want to spend hours alone with him. Nope, working would be the best thing for both of them.

Merri walked over to him and hugged him before giving him a quick kiss on the cheek. "Unless she told you *in words*, you're assuming, and you shouldn't do that. Ask her. You're married now. She's a wonderful person. Make the best of this."

"We both know what to expect from this marriage." He'd given Merri and Tobias a shortened version of his and Alison's arrangement when he'd invited them to the wedding.

"Are you sure about that?" Merri gently touched his nose.

"Hey." He pulled his head away. "That hurts."

"I bet." Tobias laughed, taking Merri's hand. "I have to say this is the first wedding I've been to where the bride broke the groom's nose."

"Me too." Adrian walked into the room. "I'm so glad I filmed this."

"It's not broken." He touched it carefully. "And you'd better not release that. I'll sue your ass."

"Too late." Adrian plopped his large body onto a chair.

"Good night. See you online." Tobias laughed and turned to Adrian. "Email me that link."

"Will do." Adrian pulled out his phone as Tobias and Merri left.

"Delete it," he said.

"I can't. You know the Internet. Once it's out there, it's out there." Adrian grinned as he took a sip of his beer.

"Alison is going to be embarrassed."

"Nah. She'll think it's funny. Trust me. I asked Ellie before I uploaded it."

"She'll laugh but she won't think it's funny. So, remove it."

"Married"—Adrian looked at his watch—"six hours and you already know her better than her best friend."

"Take it down." He wasn't in the mood for Adrian's shit.

"I'd heard marriage made people grumpy, but this happened fast." Adrian tapped the screen of his phone. "Okay. It's down but I can't swear it isn't anywhere else."

"Is Ellie still with her?" He was beginning to wonder if the other woman was going to spend the night.

"Yeah, but don't worry. Ellie told me to give her thirty minutes and then come and get her. We'll be gone soon."

"No hurry." He didn't have to see Adrian's face to know he'd screwed that up. This was his wedding night. He should be eager to be alone with is bride even under these circumstances.

"You'd better not hurt her." Adrian's tone was serious for one of the first times that Harker had ever heard.

"She knows what this is." He knew that Alison had told Ellie everything which meant Adrian knew too.

"It doesn't matter. Things change. Feelings change."

"Not for us. We respect each other and get along. That's enough."

"That's bullshit. That's enough for what your relationship was but not what it is now. She's your wife."

"Not really."

"You said the vows."

"Yes, technically she's my wife for the moment."

"And you think you'll just walk away after living with her for a year, sharing a bed and having a child? You're not as smart as I thought."

CHAPTER 21: Alison

"Why are you so nervous?" Ellie grabbed Alison's arm to stop her from pacing. "It's just sex."

"With Harker." Alison grimaced. "The man is probably going to be barking orders at me the entire time."

"I'm sure he won't." Ellie took Alison's hands. "He'll take one look at you and—"

"He'll say," Alison mimicked Harker's voice. "Alison, what are you doing? Stop making those noises. And for God's sake stop talking and do what I'm paying you to do."

"There's no way he'll say those things." Ellie laughed.

"I bet he does." Alison giggled. "He already has said those exact things to me many times." She looked around Harker's large bedroom. "I need another drink." She started for the door and stopped, glancing down at the lingerie she wore. It was a present from Ellie, and it was beautiful. White satin and lace that barely skimmed the top of her thighs with a low-cut neckline and lace covering her breasts. She also wore a robe of sorts. It matched the lingerie but was completely see through. The entire outfit was stunning. Too bad it was on her body. Her small breasts and wide hips didn't do the garment justice. "Go get me a drink. Even though almost everyone is gone, I can't walk around the house like this."

"I think you've had enough. You don't want to pass out on your wedding night."

"Actually, that sounds like an excellent idea." Alison tried not to laugh when she pictured Harker's face when he saw her passed out on his bed. "Harker probably wouldn't mind. At least I'd be quiet. He hates it when I talk all the time and I always talk a lot when

I'm nervous and"—she grabbed Ellie's hands—"I'm so nervous. Please, please, please get me another drink."

"Relax. You know him. He's a good guy. You even like him."

Alison snorted. "As a boss not as a...man with a penis."

"That's a new way of referring to a husband. They should add that to the ceremony." Ellie lowered her voice to sound like a man. "Alison, do you take this man as your lawfully wedded man with a penis." She giggled. "That'd get some attention."

"I can't believe I'm married." Alison dropped onto the bed. "I have a husband. What am I supposed to do with a husband? I know what most women do with husbands, but I can't. It's Harker."

Ellie sat next to her. "It's just sex, Alison. You've been saying you need to get laid and now you will. On a regular basis. Be happy." She hugged her friend and kissed her on the cheek before standing. "Call me tomorrow unless you're too busy getting lucky."

"Don't go." Alison clung to her hand. "As soon as you leave, he'll come in here."

"That's the point. It's already late. Everyone else left hours ago." Ellie squeezed her hand. "Relax and enjoy it. He's a man. You're a woman. It'll be fun." She tried to pull her hand free, but Alison wasn't ready to be alone with her husband, Gus Barker.

"Please get me another drink. Then you can go. Please."

"You don't—"

"I do. I really, really need another drink."

Ellie sighed. "Let go of my hand and I'll get you another drink but then Adrian and I are leaving."

"You know, the two of you should stay. We'll make a fun night of it. The four of us can play cards or watch movies."

"Harker would kill us both. He's been staring at you like a starving man all day."

Alison made a gagging noise. "It's Harker. I just don't see him that way."

"You should open your eyes because the man is gorgeous."

"No, Adrian is gorgeous."

"He is but Harker has that dark, brooding look that should be making your panties disappear." Ellie studied her friend. "Why isn't he?"

"I don't know. I guess because I know him. He's not my type at all."

"How can he not be your type? Everyone loves dark and brooding."

"I thought the same thing when I met him, but he was my boss."

"Who you practically lived with. You mean you never once thought about what it would be like if the two of you hooked up?"

"No. Bosses are off limits. Plus as I got to know him, I put him in the friend zone." She wouldn't admit this to Ellie because her friend would argue but men like Harker didn't date women like her—too smart, too talkative with little breasts and a big butt. "And now I only see him as that gruff, barking, grumpy guy. You know, the old guy who yells at the neighborhood kids to get off his yard."

"You need your eyesight, or your head examined. Harker is hot and he's all yours." Ellie grinned. "You're going to get to see his cum face."

"Oh, gross." Alison leaned forward, slapping her friend's arm. "Thanks. Now I can't stop wondering what he'll look like."

"You won't have to wonder for long."

"It's not funny." Alison laughed. "Go get me that drink and make it a double."

"A double? No way. You're already plastered." Ellie left the bedroom.

"You suck as a friend," she yelled at the closed door and then flopped back onto the mattress. She was on Harker's bed. She sat up. "This is the biggest bed I've ever seen. Who needs a bed this big? You could fit at least five or six adults on here. Why would anyone even want a bed this big? What does he do in here?" She stood, eyeing the bed. "This thing is huge. They must've built the bed in here but the mattress...How did it even fit—"

"Trust me, it'll fit and it's not huge, but it is larger than normal," said Harker.

She spun around at his deep, rich voice. "What are you...You scared me." She swallowed as he closed the door. She'd never noticed how big he was. He had to be at least six foot tall with broad shoulders that tapered to a narrow waist and hips.

"Sorry." His dark gaze wandered over her.

"Ah...Ellie is coming back any minute." She tugged her robe closer to her neck, not that it'd do much good. There wasn't much to it, but it made her feel safer. Safer? She wasn't scared of Harker. Was she? She had no idea what she felt at this moment—her nerves tangled with something. It couldn't be desire. This was Harker. Barker. Gus. It had to be the alcohol, making the room seem hot and small with him inside it.

"No, she isn't. She and Adrian left." He walked to a cabinet and opened the door, displaying a small but well stocked bar.

"You have a bar in your room? I could've been drinking all this time." She moved closer to him without thinking. "Why didn't you tell me you had a bar in your bedroom?" It seemed like something she should know.

"Do you want me to answer all your questions?" He sent her an amused look over his shoulder. "Or just a few?"

"There weren't that many." Here came the jabs about how much she talked.

"Okay. Yes, I obviously have a bar in my bedroom, and it never crossed my mind to tell you about it." He handed her a drink. "I would've gladly shown it to you if you'd ever given me the slightest hint that you were interested in seeing my bedroom."

"Why would I want to see your bedroom? You were my boss." She took a big gulp of her drink.

"We worked many late nights together." He poured himself a drink. "Stranger things have happened between two"—his eyes roamed down her body again—"attractive adults."

"Please." She gulped down her drink, trying to chase away the tingly feelings his dark eyes and husky voice were causing. "You would've said something like, Alison, you don't need to see my bedroom. You need to work. Stop dallying and get working."

"I assure you." He took the glass from her and put it on the cabinet. "I wouldn't have said any of those things if you'd wanted to see my bedroom." He took a sip of his drink, his eyes on her breasts.

"Right. Maybe not at first." She moved away from him. It was getting hot over there. "But then things would've been awkward between us and I don't do one-night stands."

"Never? You don't have even one passionate mistake in your past."

"No. Okay. Maybe one but it doesn't really count."

"Why is that?" He leaned against the dresser near the bar.

"It was college. Nothing that happens in college counts."

"Did you have sex?" His voice grew deeper, seeming to make that last word a living entity in the room.

"Ah, yeah." She swallowed. "Kind of."

"Kind of?" His brow rose. "What is kind of sex? Oral? Anal?"

"No. Oral isn't sex and no, no way for anal."

"You've never..."

"No and I don't want to."

"Are you sure?" His eyes seemed to glow with a promise of pleasure she'd never imagined.

She opened her mouth, but the words wouldn't come out. She coughed to clear her throat. "Yes. I mean. Yes, I'm sure that I don't want to."

"I'll have to see if I can change your mind." He put his drink down and took a step toward her.

"Wait." She stepped back. "Let's talk about this."

"I don't think we need to talk right now."

"I do. I mean we're married, but we're only married for the purposes of procreation, right?"

"Yes." He continued toward her.

"Then those things aren't necessary." She backed away again.

"Those things?"

"You know." Her words slipped out as a whisper. "Oral. Anal."

"So, you don't want me to bury my face between your legs and kiss you until you come."

An image of large hands gripping her thighs and holding them apart as a dark head lowered between them and a mouth, hot and wet, kissing her intimately made her melt until he looked up and barked orders at her. A bubble of nervous laughter rolled up her throat and burst from her lips followed by another and another.

"I really don't see what's so funny?" Harker's dry tone made her laugh harder.

"I'm...I'm sorry. No. It's not funny." She dropped onto the bed laughing.

"Please explain it to me. I could use a laugh today."

"I'm sorry. It's just...you...no, not you." She took a deep breath. "The idea of you...and me...and you barking at me when you're...doing that." She waved her hand by the tops of her thighs. "I can hear you now." She lowered her voice to imitate him. "Alison, I need a timeline for your completion. I need to see your project plan, so I know when you'll finish." Another burst of laughter flew from her.

"I see." He turned and strode toward the door.

"Wait. I'm sorry. I won't laugh. It's not funny. I just..." She giggled and his back stiffened before he slammed the door behind him.

CHAPTER 22: Alison

It took several minutes but Alison finally got her laughter under control. She was an asshole. Harker had been trying to be sexy, and she'd laughed in his face. The alcohol in her stomach gurgled. She'd messed up and the worst part was now she had to find him and apologize. He was a nice guy and she'd hurt him.

She left the room and headed for his office. She'd apologize and maybe they could have a wedding night. She bit her lip to keep from giggling at the thought of kissing him. He'd probably tell her she was doing it wrong.

No, damn it. She had to stop thinking like that or she'd laugh again, and she wasn't sure their marriage—she giggled—the sham that it was, could withstand that.

She stumbled down the hallway and knocked on his office door, but he didn't answer. She opened it and the room was empty. He'd been in the library earlier tonight.

She headed across the house and stopped in the doorway. The room was dark except for the light from a small lamp on the desk. He stood with his back to her, staring out the window into the night. His dark hair brushed against the collar of his white shirt. Too bad she didn't have her phone. It would've been a great picture—the dark night matching his hair and the moon as white as his shirt. It could've been a horror movie if he'd left on his bloodstained one. She snorted back a laugh.

"What do you want?" He didn't turn around.

"I'm sorry." She took a small step toward him. "I didn't mean to laugh."

He didn't reply.

"I couldn't help it. I've had too much to drink."

"Do not use alcohol as an excuse." He spun around, his dark eyes unreadable. "Alcohol and drugs exaggerate who we are and what we think. They don't make us do or say things that aren't already inside of us."

"I know but I am sorry."

"Me too."

"I...I'm really nervous. I talk too much when I'm nervous."

"Only then?"

She made a face at him. "You knew I talked a lot when you agreed to this."

"But I didn't know you laughed a lot." A glint of humor sparkled in his dark eyes.

"I laugh all the time. You've even made comments."

"Yes, but you weren't laughing at me."

"Keep believing that," she joked.

His lips turned up in a small grin. "Is this a common thing with you? Laughing at me?" He took a step toward her.

Her nerves started arcing again. "I don't know if I'd say common, but I wouldn't call it uncommon either."

"Please tell me. What do you find so amusing about me?" He stalked closer. "Many find my dry wit entertaining but no one has ever burst into a fit of laughter over it."

"I bet not."

"You don't have to be that sure," he mumbled.

"Sorry." She laughed. "I meant that I usually laugh at how cranky you are."

"I'm not that grumpy."

"Please. You're always yelling at me. Every day I hear, *Alison, get in here. Alison, you're late. Alison—*"

"That's not true."

"Uh, yeah, it is. I even created this random generator of the twenty most common Barkerisms. Every day I click the button to see which one you'll say. If you say that one, then I do it again." She giggled. "One day I played Harker's Barker-Meter thirteen—"

"Harker's Barker-Meter? You wrote a program about me." He stopped in front of her.

"I probably shouldn't have told you that." She looked up at him.

The moonlight put his face in shadows and suddenly he didn't seem like the same man she'd known for months. His shirt glowed in the light and there was so much white. His chest was muscular, lean and all male and it was right there in front of her.

"No, you probably shouldn't have." He leaned down, his mouth only inches from hers. "Now, I'll have to reprimand you for messing around on the job."

"Oh my god. That's the one it picked for today. I never thought you'd say it. Not today." She burst out laughing and her head tipped back, slamming into his nose again.

"Shit. Fuck." He backed away his hand over his face.

"Oh, oh. I'm so sorry." This was a disaster. She felt horrible, but she laughed harder. "You're bleeding again." It wasn't as much this time, but a few drops colored his clean shirt. "Let me help." She moved toward him.

"Stay the fuck away from me." He side-stepped her and headed for the door.

"Where are you going?"

"Away from you." He strode down the hallway.

Alison heard a door open, and then slam shut, followed by the sound of the garage door opening and closing. She dropped onto the couch, holding her stomach and laughing. This wasn't funny. It really wasn't, but he was so predictable, and he was her husband who'd just left her on their wedding night. Tears ran down her cheeks and she blamed them on the laughter.

CHAPTER 23: Harker

"Harker, good to see you." Katie, one of the waitresses at La Petite Mort Club, stopped next to him at the bar. "Is that blood on your shirt?"

"It's nothing. Sit." He pushed out a chair. "Keep me company."

"You know I can't. I have tables and customers to wait on."

"Quit and spend the night with me." He was half joking. He liked her. She was cute with short, reddish-brown hair. She reminded him of a pixie.

"No can do. Then I'd have to do that for all my favorite customers and I'm not quite ready to hang up my tray"—she waved her cocktail tray—"for a bracelet." The one thing that identified a Pleasure Associate from everyone else at the Club.

"Good. You shouldn't." He'd happily fuck her if she were a Pleasure Associate but a woman like her didn't fuck for fun. She was a marrying kind of gal and he already had a wife. He should've picked Katie. She wouldn't have laughed him out of his wedding bed.

"Oh, now you're hurting my feelings," she teased.

"Trust me, I'll be your best client if you ever switch jobs."

"Oh Harker, you'd tire of me in no time just like you do every one of your subs." She put her hand on her chest. "And I don't want to be left heartbroken and horny."

"I should pay you to talk to a woman I know." He laughed. This was what he'd needed. Someone to appreciate him as a man.

"Oh, poor baby. Is that why you're drinking alone tonight? Your new conquest isn't interested."

"You could say that."

"My money is on you. If you want her, you'll win her over and if you don't, then it's her loss."

It soothed his pride until Alison's laughing face flashed through his mind. It was time to change the subject. He didn't need to get more depressed. "Have you finished those classes yet? I may have a clerical position opening soon."

"No. I quit. I had to pick up some extra shifts. My sister is living with me. Parents kicked her out. She's pregnant."

"Oh. I'm sorry to hear that."

Katie shrugged. "I had to let her stay with me. She's family."

His family hadn't felt that way. "When you finish college, let me know. I'll find an opening for you and I'll pay you well." Loyalty and honesty were commodities that were worth every penny.

"Thank you. I really appreciate it. I hope to start classes again as soon as my sister finds a job." She smiled warmly at him, her eyes darting over his shoulder. "I gotta go. Customers are waiting."

"Hold on." He pulled out his wallet and handed her several hundred dollars.

"What's this for? I didn't even bring you a drink."

"It'll help with your bills."

"I can't take this. If I'd waited on you maybe but—"

"I insist." He squeezed her hand. "You made me laugh on the shittiest day of my life. That's worth at least this much."

"Thank you." Her eyes filled with tears.

"Thank you."

"I think your night is about to get better." She kissed his cheek and then hurried off to wait on her customers.

"Hello, Harker." A warm, throaty voice that he hadn't heard in a long time whispered in his ear as a small hand ran across his shoulder, nails scraping slightly and making his balls tighten.

"Dahlia." He turned. His night was definitely looking up.

"Is that blood?" She ran her finger across his shirt.

"Yeah. It's nothing." He didn't want to talk about the blood, his wife or his wedding. "What brings you back to the states?"

"Boredom mainly." She sat next to him, crossing her long legs.

He hadn't seen her in almost two years, but she looked as beautiful as ever with her black hair and even darker eyes. She'd been his sub for over a year. She'd had to move for business, and they'd parted as friends.

"I find that hard to believe. You make your own fun." His eyes dropped to her breasts which were displayed nicely in her low-cut pale green dress.

"It's true but I'm also here on business." She waved over the bartender. "Vodka on the rocks."

"On me."

"Thank you." She touched his arm. "I'd hoped to see you here and thought we could have some fun while I'm in town." Her knee bumped his as her fingers traced along his sleeve. "I missed you, Harker. The men in France have wonderful accents but"—she frowned slightly—"they don't punish me like I want."

His dick was hard and ready to play and why shouldn't he? His marriage wasn't real, and his bride didn't even think of him as a man.

"Do you want to go to a playroom?" Her hand rested on his thigh, her fingers tracing lightly over his cock. "I could stand to release some tension and it feels like you could too." She touched his face with her other hand. "You look tired. I bet you're working too hard again. You need to have some fun."

"You're right. I do." He grabbed her hand and kissed her palm.

"Then let's go play." She leaned closer and kissed him. Her lips were soft and her taste familiar but strange after so long.

Her tongue slipped into his mouth as her hand squeezed his dick. He groaned, tangling his fingers in her hair and holding her still for his kiss. It'd been too long since he'd fucked. He'd been working a lot and spending too many nights deciding if Alison were the right woman to have his child. Then, even when he'd had spare time to come to the Club, he hadn't found anyone who'd interested him but now Dahlia was back.

He broke the kiss and stood, taking her hand and leading her toward the playrooms. He'd be damned if he was going to be celibate on his wedding night.

CHAPTER 24: Harker

"It looks like playrooms four and nine are available. What are you in the mood for tonight, Dahlia? The spanking bench and bed or the hoist?" Harker kissed her hand.

"You're the master." She ran her fingernail down his chest. "You decide."

"Mr. Harker, one moment please." Damon, one of the bouncers, strode toward him.

"Excuse me." He kissed her hand again and turned toward the bouncer, his nerves humming. There was no reason for this interruption. He'd paid his dues. They were both consenting adults. "Yes, Damon?"

"Ethan would like to speak with you." The bouncer nodded at Dahlia.

"Hello, Damon." Dahlia smiled at him and then teased, "Harker, please tell me you haven't done something to get kicked out of the Club?"

"Hardly." He had a pretty good idea of the reason for this delay. Ethan might own the sex club, but the man was an old-fashioned romantic at heart. "Tell him I'll talk to him later." He tugged on Dahlia's hand. "The spanking bench would suit me perfectly tonight." He needed to take out his frustration on someone and she liked it hard.

"Sorry, sir." Damon stepped in front of the door. "Ethan said to insist."

"Bloody hell." He dropped Dahlia's hand. "Go inside and get ready for me. I'll be right there."

"Actually," Ethan strode into the hallway. "Why don't the two of us go into the playroom. Dahlia can wait out here with Damon."

"Ethan." She gave him a warm hug. "I'd hoped to see you tonight."

"It's nice to see you again, Dahlia." Ethan smiled at her.

She touched his cheek. "You're looking even more haggard than Harker." Her hand trailed down his arm as she glanced over her shoulder. "Master, may I ask him to join us?"

"Sure." He and Ethan had shared women before but that was years ago when Ethan had been fun. Now, the man spent more time alone in his office than fucking in the Club.

"Thank you, but not this time." Ethan kissed her cheek. "Give us a moment, please."

"Sure. I'll wait at the bar."

"Not necessary," said Ethan. "This should only take a minute." He walked into the playroom.

Harker was confused. If Ethan were going to lecture him on being here without his wife on his wedding day, then removing Dahlia from the picture would be the most logical thing to do. Maybe this had to do with something else. He followed the other man into the room, closing the door behind him. "Is there a problem with my account?"

"What the fuck are you doing here?"

His first assumption had been the right one. "I don't need to explain myself or my actions to you."

"Of course not but I consider you a friend."

"How wonderful for me."

Ethan gave him a dirty look. "Go home. Get back in bed with your wife."

"No." If only it were that simple. "Is there anything else?"

"You're not going to listen to a word I say, are you?"

"Send Dahlia in when you leave." Harker walked to the small bar in the room and poured himself and Dahlia a drink. Ethan could go fuck himself. He deserved this and it wasn't like Alison would care.

"Sure." Ethan gave him a disgusted look. "Come see me when you're done." He strode to the door and opened it. "Dahlia, he's all yours."

She walked into the room and stopped, so close to Ethan that her breasts brushed against his arm. "You sure you won't join us?"

"No, thank you." Ethan glanced at Harker a smug look on his face. "But you may want to congratulate him on his wedding."

"Mother fucker." Harker's fist tightened on his glass.

She laughed. "He doesn't believe in marriage." Her eyes darted to him and the laughter fled. "Harker?"

"It's not a real marriage." He could salvage this. She was logical.

"It's true? You're married?" she asked.

"Yes, but it's temporary." He moved toward her. "I want a child. She wants a business." He ignored Ethan's snort. "As soon as she has my child we'll divorce." He took her hand. "I swear."

"You're serious. It's not a real marriage?" She turned toward Ethan and Harker wanted to shake her. He'd been her master. Her dom. She should believe him.

"That's what he told me too," said Ethan.

"But you don't believe him?"

Harker met Ethan's gaze over her head.

"I believe he thinks that's the case."

"There's nothing to *think*. It's fact. It's in the contract." He tugged on Dahlia's hand. "Look at me. If I were truly married, I wouldn't be here with you. You know me. I'm not like that. I was faithful to you." She was still unsure but there was a softness to her gaze that hadn't been there a minute ago. He could fix this. "Go away, Ethan. Dahlia and I need to talk."

Ethan paused but when Dahlia didn't say anything, he nodded. "Okay, but you may want to ask him why he's wearing a wedding ring if this marriage is such a sham."

"I forgot to take it off."

"Forgot?" asked Ethan. "I'd think it'd feel foreign on your finger since you just got married this afternoon."

"Today? You got married today?" Dahlia almost screeched and Harker knew exactly how she felt.

CHAPTER 25: Harker

Harker stormed into Ethan's office. "Why the fuck did you do that you meddlesome piece of shit?" He'd done his best to salvage his night, but Dahlia had refused to listen to him.

"Sit down and have a drink." Ethan was on the couch watching the Club through the monitors.

"I should kick the shit out of you." He plopped down on a chair and grabbed the drink Ethan had prepared for him.

"I'd like to see you try." Ethen shot him a look. "It'd give me a good reason to kick your ass like you deserve. What the fuck are you doing here anyway?"

"Trying to get laid on my wedding night." He hadn't meant to admit that, but it'd been like a blister waiting to pop.

"Isn't that what your bride is for?" Ethan turned away from the monitors to focus on him.

"That's what I thought but I was mistaken."

"She refused? I thought she'd agreed to have your kid. Did she think you were doing that through a clinic or something?"

"No. She understood. It was all in the contract."

"Fucking women. Drink up." Ethan slid the bottle of bourbon toward Harker. "It's so unfair. If women want sex, we fall all over ourselves to be first in line to fuck them."

"I know." He tossed back his drink.

"They have those glorious pussies and can get cock whenever they want. it." Ethan leaned back. "Maybe we men should decide to hold out. Make them all beg. Turn the tables."

"That'd be perfect. The women of the world chasing us men. Begging us to fuck them." He could see Alison now, kneeling before him begging for his cock. His eyes met Ethan's and they both burst out laughing. "Not one of us would make it past the first offer."

"Nope. Not one." Ethan refilled his glass. "Shame though."

"Yeah, it is."

They sat in silence for few minutes.

"So, what did you do?" asked Ethan.

"Nothing."

"Come on. A woman doesn't refuse to fuck her husband on her wedding night."

"She didn't refuse."

"I'm confused." Ethan frowned.

Harker's jaw tensed. "She...she laughed."

"She laughed?" Ethan pointed to Harker's crotch. "At your—"

"No. We hadn't gotten that far."

"Oh. Wow. That's good because I don't think there's any going back from that. To have a woman laugh at your di—"

"She did not laugh at my dick." He had to make that clear. He wasn't letting that rumor start.

"Right. Got it." Ethan frowned. "But...what did she laugh at because for pussy I'd let a woman laugh at almost anything—anything but my cock—and still keep going."

"She laughed at the thought of me...of us...having sex."

"Oh, fuck." Ethan's brow wrinkled. "You should've kissed her. If it's done right, there's no room for anything but lust."

"I do it right and I tried." He touched his nose. "She started laughing and busted my nose with her fucking head. She gave me a nosebleed."

"Again?"

"Again? You heard about that? Did Adrian send you the video? I'm going to kill that bastard."

"There's a video?" Ethan pulled his phone from his pocket. "I have got to see that."

"No you don't." Fuck, he'd done it now. Adrian would send the video to Ethan and Ethan would share it with everyone.

"I do. I really do." Ethan typed on his phone and then dropped it onto the couch next to him.

"If you didn't hear it from Adrian, where did—"

"Tobias and Merri came by for a drink."

"Tobias has the biggest fucking mouth."

"Yeah, but the good thing about friends like them is that you never have to worry about someone learning your secrets because you have none." Ethan laughed.

"Yeah, that's so great. I can't wait to be the next Internet sensation."

"Seriously, she was nervous. So what? You know how to deal with that."

"She's not just nervous. She doesn't see me as a man." The words tore at his inside like claws.

"Then make her."

"How the fuck am I supposed to do that? She knows I'm a man, but she's put me in the boss-friend-eunuch zone."

"Then make her see you in a different way."

"How?"

"Bring her here." Ethan's lips turned up in a half-grin. "I've seen women fuck men who they'd never look twice at anywhere else. But the Club, it's magical. The whole place is like an aphrodisiac to women and us men are the lucky dicks who get invited to play."

"I can't bring her here."

"Why not?"

"She's...she's innocent to kink."

"That's perfect. You can show her what she's missing."

His dick began to harden at the thought, but he'd never play with her, not like he did with Dahlia. Ethan must've read his mind because the other man continued.

"You don't have to drag her on stage. Just being here with you will make her see you as a man." Ethan's eyes glowed. "Tony's found another sub."

"Really?" His gaze locked with Ethan's. "Who? He's particularly picky."

"A new member. I doubt she'll hold his interest for long, but I heard he's ready to take her to the stage."

"When?" Seeing Tony perform made all the women horny as fuck. It was always a disappointment when he was between subs because everyone got laid for free after Tony's show.

"Not sure. I can talk to him. I'll see if he'd be willing to wait for you and your bride to be here."

"Yeah. Do it." He wanted to go home and drag Alison here, but she'd be passed out by now.

"What day should I tell him?"

"Friday."

"That's almost a week from now."

"I know but this weekend isn't going to work. Alison was pretty drunk. She's going to be hung over tomorrow."

"Weekdays are good for fucking too."

"No shit, but we've got a lot of work. It has to be Friday. And save me a room. I think we'll spend the night."

"Got it. I don't know if Tony will wait that long but I'm sure I can talk him into performing again."

CHAPTER 26: Alison

Alison groaned and pulled the pillow over her head to block that annoying sound. Her phone rang again. She grabbed it from the nightstand. "Hello." Her voice sounded like she'd gargled with gravel.

"Alison? Did I wake you?" asked Ellie.

"Yes." She wanted to go back to sleep. Correction. She wanted to drink a gallon of water and then go back to sleep. Her head still pounded but at least she didn't feel nauseous anymore.

"Wow. It's almost three in the afternoon. I guess I don't have to ask how last night went."

"Three?" She glanced toward the window, but the drapes were thick and pulled tightly together. The room would be in total darkness if she hadn't left the bathroom light on so Harker wouldn't trip when he'd come home...except he hadn't come to bed.

"Yeah. Three in the afternoon. You never sleep late. You must be worn out." The teasing tone in Ellie's voice made Alison want to scream, except that'd make her head explode. "I knew it. I knew he'd be good in bed. All that dark brooding angst."

"I can hear you, Ellie," yelled Adrian.

"Oh...I mean, I'm sure he was good but not as good as Adrian."

"That's better," he said, a smug tone in his voice.

"If he were half as good as Adrian, you'd be so lucky," said Ellie.

"Half? Why do I only get half as good?" Alison sat up, rubbing her eyes. "Don't I deserve as good as Adrian?"

"Of course, you do."

"But good luck with that." Adrian's voice was louder. He must've moved closer to Ellie. "Because there aren't many guys...I mean, any guys as good as me. I'm a very considerate lover."

"Yes, you are dear, but this is about Alison," said Ellie.

"No, you guys go on." She didn't want to talk about last night. "I really don't have much to say."

"You? Nothing to say. That's impossible," said Adrian.

Alison pulled the phone a little away from her ear at the sound of a scuffle.

"Adrian, what are you doing?" yelled Ellie. "Give me back the phone."

"As soon as I put this on speaker. If Alison is without words, I have got to hear this. Did you break his nose again?"

"I didn't break his nose and Ellie, take me off speakerphone."

"I can't Alison," said Ellie. "He won't give me the phone."

Alison was pretty sure Ellie wasn't even trying to get it. "Adrian, I'm not kidding. Give her the phone and take me off speaker."

"Nope. You owe me," said Adrian.

"I owe you. For what?" If anything, Adrian owed her for helping him and Ellie get together.

"For that nightmare of a phone call on the way to Ellie's parents' house."

"I was trying to help you."

"You were eviscerating me with every word."

"Oh please, it wasn't that bad." She'd thought it was fun.

"You told me to watch pornos so I could learn to be better in bed." Adrian's words dripped with disgust.

"So? There's nothing wrong with that." She'd done that herself a few times.

"Porn is art. You should watch it for appreciation not education."

"You can do both. Ask Ellie." Alison laughed.

"Me? You're the one who gave me the idea," said Ellie. "Speaking of educational experiences, did your husband teach you any new tricks?"

"Ellie's the reason I suggested that." She had to deflect. "She's the one who said you weren't good in bed."

"That's true," Adrian's voice grew serious. "You did lie, Ellie."

"And I apologized and"—there was the sound of a soft kiss—"I'm making it up to you."

"Not fast enough. You were quite a bitch."

"Hey!" laughed Ellie.

"What?" he teased. "It's true but I love you anyway."

"Ahh. I love you too, Adrian." Another soft kiss.

Alison wanted to puke and cry. It was so sweet, and she was happy for her friend, but she wanted that too. Instead she got a marriage for hire or more accurately a marriage for baby.

"But enough about us," said Ellie. "Alison must not want to talk about last night because she keeps changing the subject."

"You are astute," she mumbled.

"And persistent."

"I could hang up." She should do that.

"Go ahead. I'll drive over there and then we'll be having this conversation with your new hubby as well as with Adrian."

"Fine." Her friend was dogged enough to do exactly what she said. "I don't know how Harker is in bed because we didn't sleep together."

"You didn't...It was your wedding night," said Adrian.

"I know what night it was." Honestly, these two were annoying.

"Are you using the word sleep literally or figuratively?" asked Ellie.

"We didn't have sex. Are you happy?"

"You didn't? Why not? It was your wedding night," said Ellie.

"You don't have to keep repeating that."

"Why didn't you have sex?" Ellie asked again.

"I don't want to talk about it."

"Adrian, get the keys. We're going over—"

"Don't. I'll tell you but this is so embarrassing."

"Oh, this is going to be so good." Adrian must've moved right next to the phone because his voice was much louder.

"I laughed."

"At his—"

"No." She interrupted Adrian before he could say it. "I didn't see that."

"Was the room dark?" asked Ellie.

"No. We didn't get that far."

"Then what did you laugh at?" asked Adrian.

"At the thought of us...You know. I was drunk and then I went to apologize and...and...I laughed again and hit him in the nose."

"Again?" asked both Adrian and Ellie.

"Yes, again." She really had to apologize to Harker.

"Poor guy," muttered Adrian. "That had to be the worse wedding and wedding night ever."

"I know. I feel horrible. His nose bled again and then he left."

"He left? The room? Or the house?" asked Ellie.

"Both. He didn't come home until really late and he slept in the library." She'd woken early the next morning and had gone into the kitchen for some water. She'd been worried about him when she'd realized that he wasn't in bed with her. She'd searched the house and had found him stretched out on the couch in the library. "I feel terrible about this whole thing. What should I do?" She was pretty sure that the blanket she'd covered him with wouldn't be enough to make him forgive her.

"Apologize," said Ellie. "Explain that you were drunk and nervous."

"And then get on your knees and apologize by sucking his dick," added Adrian.

"Adrian." There was the sound of a soft slap and laughter from Ellie.

"What? It'll work. A man can't stay mad at a woman when her mouth is full of his dick. It's physically impossible."

"You are not helping." Ellie laughed harder and then cleared her throat. "Harker is a reasonable man. Talk to him."

"Harker? Reasonable?" Alison almost choked. "That man isn't the least bit reasonable. You do things his way or not at all."

"I think you covered the not at all," muttered Adrian.

"Ellie's right. You aren't helping."

"Apologize to him," said Ellie. "He'll listen and he'll be super horny."

"I doubt that," laughed Adrian.

"Why?" asked both women.

"Ah...shit...no reason."

"Spill, Adrian," said Ellie.

"Okay, but I don't know anything," he said. "I'm just guessing. You both understand that, right?"

"Yes," said Ellie. "Now, talk."

Alison's fingers squeezed the phone. She wasn't sure she wanted to hear this.

"Okay. Like I said, I know nothing. I'm assuming that since he didn't get laid at home on his wedding night, he probably went somewhere else to take care of that."

"Is that what you'd do?" asked Ellie.

Alison almost shivered from the ice in her friend's tone.

"No but I love you. Harker and Alison have a different kind of relationship." Adrian's voice lowered, "But I would be pissed if I didn't get laid on my wedding night. I know we men aren't supposed to admit that we expect sex, but we do. Take a woman out to a nice restaurant and dancing—we expect sex."

"A woman doesn't have to put out because you buy her dinner," said Ellie.

"Of course not," said Adrian. "But that doesn't mean we don't expect her to. I'm not saying we should force her or anything but if she...fails to live up to our expectations often enough we look elsewhere. That's why I chased after you so much. I knew you put out."

"You're an asshole," said Ellie.

"Ouch. Stop it. Your elbow is pointy," said Adrian.

"And you're a jerk," said Ellie. "I'm sure Harker didn't go anywhere to have sex."

"I know he didn't," she said.

"How? Did you follow him?" asked Ellie.

"No, but monogamy is in our contract and Harker won't break the contract."

"So was having sex, right?" asked Adrian "Sounds to me like you broke the contract first."

"Shit." Had she? "No. I didn't refuse him."

"You may as well have. You laughed and that probably made his balls tuck back into his body for protection," said Adrian. "But what does it matter if he did go out and get laid? It's not like you care for the guy."

He was right. It shouldn't matter but it did. "It matters because he's my husband and while we're married, I expect him to be faithful."

"Then you better get over those giggles and start putting out. Harker isn't the kind of guy to go without," said Adrian.

"How do you know?" asked Alison. "Have the two of you been hanging out or something?"

"Or something," he said. "When we met at the bar on New Year's Eve, I didn't recognize him, but I saw him at the Club a few times after that. He's a member."

"What club?" asked Alison.

"Uhm...uh..." Adrian stammered.

"You mean, La Petite Mort Club." Alison couldn't believe that grumpy, dry Harker was a member of the premiere sex club in the area.

"Yeah. I never saw him with anyone. He was there having a few drinks and talking but according to my friend Mitch, Harker used to go there a lot a few years ago and he never lacked for company."

"Did you know this, Ellie?" Her friend was too quiet.

"Adrian mentioned it but that was after you'd already had your mind set on marrying him. Why does it matter? You keep insisting that this marriage is just business."

"I don't know but it does." Her friend should've told her.

"Do you like him?" Ellie's voice was soft.

"Of course, I like him. He's a nice guy. In an irritating way."

"That's not what I meant, and you know it."

"No, I don't like him the way you're talking about."

"Then I agree with Adrian. Why do you care if he goes to La Petite Mort Club?"

"Because it's in the contract that we're both to remain monogamous until I get pregnant. We agreed. If he breaks one part, he'll break another, and I don't want to lose my partnership." That was all true, but she wasn't so sure it was the only reason.

CHAPTER 27: Harker

Harker looked up from his laptop at the soft sound of Alison's footsteps. She stood in the doorway of his private office, looking unsure. He'd never seen her like that. She was always a force of energy and movement but today she was still, her hands clasped in front of her.

Her face was pale, and she had bags under her eyes. Her hair was still damp from her shower. She wore jeans and a baggy T-shirt, not exactly the outfit of fantasies but his dick still hardened. She was meeker right now and he'd love to use this time to make her bend to his will, but he wouldn't. His pride couldn't handle another bout of her laughter. He needed to wait until they were at the Club. Then he'd help her explore her kinkier side. He only hoped she had one.

"Are you busy?" she asked.

"Always." His voice was gruff and by the widening of her eyes she probably thought he was angry not aroused. That suited him perfectly. She didn't deserve to know how she affected him since she didn't see him as a man, at least not a fuckable one.

"Oh. Sorry. I thought we could talk. Should talk."

He leaned back in his chair, watching her ramp up for full-blown Alison chatter.

"You know. About last night. I mean...it wasn't exactly...you know. It's not how I planned...what I wanted and I'm sure it's not what you wanted either and—"

"Sit." He motioned to the chair in front of his desk.

"No. I shouldn't." She edged backward a little. "You said you were busy."

"I am but I'm not going to get anything done with you yammering in the doorway."

"Right. Sorry. I can go." But she didn't move. "I just thought we should—"

"Talk. You said that."

"Yeah, I did." She stared at her hands. "But maybe we shouldn't."

"*You* don't want to talk?" That was a first.

"We can...but I thought we could...you know." She shrugged one shoulder, her eyes glancing to his and then away.

"I'm afraid I don't." He had no idea what she was talking about but that wasn't unusual.

"I thought we could...you know." She stressed the last two words.

"I really don't."

"Have sex," she whispered.

"Now?" After she'd laughed at him and tried to kill him by shoving his nose through his brain...twice.

"Yeah. I want to apologize for last night. I didn't mean to lau—"

"Stop."

"But I want to apologize."

"You don't need to say it. I heard enough about it last night."

"From who? Where did you go?" Her meekness disappeared fast as she stepped into the room. "Why didn't you come to bed? I left the light on for you and I was worried when I woke."

"You had no reason to be. I've been taking care of myself for years."

"Yeah, but it was your...our wedding night."

"If you were so worried about that maybe you shouldn't have drunk yourself into a stupor."

"I was nervous."

"About what?" His temper rose like a volcano.

"About us. The marriage. Sex."

"Oh, so suddenly you're a virgin again?"

"No but we've never had sex."

"You have to get plastered before your first time with every man or am I special?" He knew the answer to that and wished he hadn't asked.

"It's not...I never..."

"Yes, I'm quite aware that you don't think of me as a man." There he'd said it. It shouldn't hurt so much once it was out in the open–again–but it did. It ripped into him like the words had teeth.

"No." She stepped closer. "I know you're a man but...I never thought of...I don't know. I...I want to do it now though. Isn't that enough?"

"No." It was for his dick but not his pride.

"No?" She seemed shocked.

He almost laughed. He should tell Ethan of his victory. He'd made a stand for all men. She wanted sex and he was refusing her. Funny, he didn't feel victorious.

"But...but we're married. You want a kid."

"Maybe later when I work myself up for it." If she came around his desk, she'd see his lie. He was more than up for it.

"Oh...right...sorry." She self-consciously touched her hair.

He felt some vindication that she now knew how he'd felt last night–unwanted, undesirable, and unfuckable.

"I...I guess I'm going to go do some work."

"Good idea." He refused to feel bad about her hurt feelings when he had his own wounds to lick.

CHAPTER 28: Alison

Alison glanced at the time on her laptop as her stomach growled for about the hundredth time. It was almost ten p.m. She'd spent the entire day hiding in her office and she'd be more than happy to spend the rest of the night there except she was starving. Her stomach grumbled again. "Be quiet. You win." She closed her laptop and stood. "I have to face the asshole sooner or later. It's stupid to sit in here and starve."

She left the office and walked down the long hallway to the private section of Harker's house. She opened the door, sighing with relief when he wasn't sitting in the living room, a frown on his stupid face. She quietly made her way to the kitchen, listening for any sound of HIM. She didn't want to see him again. Ever. She'd wasted enough time feeling sorry for herself because of what he'd said. He was always bossy and arrogant, but he'd never been cruel until today.

She opened the refrigerator and pulled out some of the leftovers from their wedding luncheon. The little bit of food she'd eaten had been delicious. She grabbed two plates and began filling them with a wide array of finger foods. She slid the plate that needed to be warmed into the microwave and put the other one on the table. She grabbed a bottle of water and sat, staring at the empty chairs. She hated eating alone. That'd been the worst thing when she'd had her own apartment.

She'd grown up always eating dinner with her family and even when she'd moved back home, she and her mom ate together whenever they could. The only times they didn't had been when she'd worked late. She'd been glad when Aunt Tiff had moved in with them. She'd felt guilty for leaving her mother to have dinner alone almost every night while she was working and eating dinner with Harker. Knowing him, he probably hadn't eaten yet. He always forgot about food when he was working.

The microwave dinged and she stood, grabbing the plate. It smelled delicious. Her stomach rumbled again. He was probably starving too but that was his problem. It wasn't her job to take care of him, except it kind of was her job. He was her husband, but he'd been mean. She wasn't the most attractive woman, but he didn't have to admit that he needed to work himself up to have sex with her.

She put the plate next to the other one and sat at the table. She'd known her marriage wouldn't be great, but she hadn't expected it to be like this, although she should have. Harker was rich and attractive in a gruff, bossy way. He was probably used to having sex with models and beautiful women. She had no idea why he wanted to make the baby the old-fashioned way. It made no sense. In vitro would be perfect. Their genes combined and he wouldn't have to work himself up to have sex with her.

She swallowed the lump of sadness that welled in her throat. He probably hadn't expected to have difficulties becoming aroused. No man wanted to even think about their little Johnson not rising to the occasion. Now that he knew it was an issue, maybe she could convince him that they should try in vitro. She stood. The best way to convince a man to do anything was to feed him or fuck him. Since the second one was off the table, that left the first. She grabbed another water and the two plates and went to find her husband.

CHAPTER 29: Alison

Since Alison carried the plates and the two bottles of water, she tapped Harker's office door with her foot.

"What?" he barked.

"It's me."

"I know it's you. We're the only two here. What I don't know is what you want."

For one second, she thought about letting him starve but this was typical Harker. His rudeness had never bothered her before, and it shouldn't bother her now in their fake marriage. "Open the door."

"You open it. I'm busy."

"Do you think I wouldn't have done that if I could. Stop being a jerk and open the door." She leaned her head near the thick door. He was grumbling but it was getting closer.

The door flew open. "And why can't you open..." His words died as his gaze landed on the plates in her hands.

She pushed past him, feeling good for the first time that day. She'd surprised him and there'd been a hint of something else in his dark eyes—gratitude maybe. "I thought you might be hungry. I know you forget to eat when you're working." She put the plates and bottles of water on his desk and began moving his laptop and papers aside. "I was starving, and all this food was so good last night."

"How would you know?" He sat behind his desk. "None of this is alcohol."

"I ate a little yesterday." She refused to let him bait her. She needed him in a good mood. In vitro was the answer to all their problems, and she didn't need his manly pride getting in the way.

"Really?" He tossed a warm cheese puff pastry into his mouth and chewed. "I didn't see you do anything but drink."

"Can we please not talk about last night. I apologized. Let's move on." She forced a smile.

"Easy for you to forget. You were drunk."

"Yes, I was and I'm sorry. Again. Okay?"

He didn't answer but he ate a bit of cheese and toasted apple.

"You aren't perfect either and I've forgiven you."

"Me? What did I do?"

She refused to admit that what he'd said that afternoon had bothered her. "You yell at me all the time. Harp on everything that I do." She ate one of the pastries filled with broccoli and cheese.

"That's work. That has nothing to do with this."

"Fine. You left last night. On our wedding night." She ate a carrot and some kind of dip that was fabulous.

"After you laughed at me."

"I..." Okay. That'd been a bad point to bring up. "Enough. Please. We're going to be living together for a long time. At least nine months."

"Nine months from conception. At the rate we're going it could take us years to get to that grand event."

"Funny you should bring that up." She took a bite of a tiny pita filled with something delicious.

"It's not funny in any way. Not even a little." He continued to eat. "Funny is the problem."

"Not funny ha-ha, but funny in a coincidental way. I was just thinking about that and I know what will make us both happy."

CHAPTER 30: Harker

"You do?" Harker knew exactly what would make him happy—bending her over his desk and fucking her. "Me too."

"Really?" She popped a bit of orange tart into her mouth, her tongue dancing across her lips to get every last bit.

He had to stifle a groan. He wanted to clean her lips, to taste her everywhere but he wasn't getting denied again. He'd take her to the Club and get her so horny she wouldn't be able to do anything but whimper for his dick.

"I bet we both have the same thing in mind." She smiled at him, a wide excited smile.

"I doubt that." He couldn't tear his eyes away from her mouth. Her pretty pink lips would look so fucking good wrapped around his dick.

"Oh, I don't know. We do think the same things a lot of times."

"For work? Yes, but this isn't work." This was pleasure, one hundred percent hot, sweaty, wet pleasure.

"But it is business. You said that yourself."

He grabbed another piece of something from the plate to keep from admitting that it wasn't only business to him. He'd be a fool to give her that weapon and he was never a fool.

"Why don't we both say what we're thinking at the count of three?"

"Let's not," he grumbled.

"Come on. If I go first and my idea is better than yours, you'll steal it."

"I would never do that." He had to fight to keep the smirk from his face. She knew him so well.

"Please." She gave him a disgusted look. "I've seen you do that to Merri and Tobias a ton of times."

"You have no idea what I was thinking and neither do they."

"Come on." She grinned. "It'll be fun."

He frowned. She was here with him instead of hiding like she'd been all day. Plus, earlier she'd approached him and had wanted to fuck. Maybe their ideas were similar.

"One. Two." She paused. "Are you going to say what you think or are you a cheater?"

"You go first."

"Write it down." She pointed at the notepad on his desk.

"What?"

"Write down your idea. Then I'll know what you were thinking." She flicked one of the pens on his desk and it rolled toward him.

"It hurts that you don't trust me."

"I know you too well."

"You do." He grinned as he grabbed the pen and the notepad. She had the innate ability to make even the most mundane tasks fun. He scribbled his idea, in less graphic terms than what was in his head, on the notepad.

"Now, give it to me." She held out her hand.

"Why?" He tore the sheet from the pad of paper and folded it.

"Because if my idea is better than yours, you'll throw it away or eat it or something."

"I won't eat it."

She wiggled her fingers. She was so damn cute—young, full of life and joy. She was everything he wasn't and everything he wanted.

"No peeking." He dropped the paper in her hand.

"Of course not." She put it down on the desk by her water.

"Now, how do you think we should resolve our issue?" he asked.

"I think we should reconsider in vitro. It's the perfect solution."

"In vitro?" The word stabbed him in the heart. She still didn't want to fuck him.

CHAPTER 31: Alison

"Uhm, yeah." Now she wished she'd kept her big mouth shut because by Harker's expression he had not been thinking of in vitro fertilization.

"No. Absolutely not." His face grew even more dour than usual.

"Why not? It'd be perfect."

"Perfect?" He snorted "How?"

"Ah...because you...we..." She refused to say he wouldn't have to work up the desire to touch her. "I could be pregnant tomorrow. Okay. Probably not tomorrow but as soon as we have the procedure."

"You could've been pregnant already."

That again. Boy, she was tired of hearing about last night. "Why are you so against in vitro? All we've done is fight since we...put sex on the table."

"We also got married, remember?" He smiled but it wasn't friendly. "Of course, you do. You hadn't even had your first drink when you almost broke my nose. How could any bride forget that?"

"That was an accident."

"Ha. I'm beginning to wonder."

"Fine. You don't like my idea but that's no reason to insult me. What was your brilliant plan?" She reached for the paper.

"No." He dove across the desk.

She snatched the paper from under his hand and pushed back her chair. "I knew you'd cheat."

"I'm not cheating." He stalked toward her. "Give me that paper."

"No." She jumped to her feet and backed away, opening the note.

"Alison, do not read that."

"I bet you had in vitro down too." Her eyes dropped to the paper. "A honeymoon?" Something happened to her heart right then that made her stomach twist. "Really? You want to go on a honeymoon? With me?" She looked up at him, but he was already walking back to his desk. She followed. "Harker?"

He stood facing the window.

"Is this a joke?"

"No." His voice was low and rough, almost vulnerable but then he cleared his throat. His shoulders shifted back as he turned and sat. "It's nothing special. Just a few nights away from here...and work. I thought we could get to know each other as people not as boss and employee." His face was stern and emotionless. It was the look he had in meetings that weren't going well. She referred to it in her head as his robot face.

"I thought we had too much work to do?" That had been his answer when Merri had asked where they were going on their honeymoon. That and the reminder that it wasn't a real wedding.

"We do so we won't be gone long. We'll leave Friday after work and be back Sunday."

"So, we're definitely going?" Maybe she should be pissed that he hadn't asked her or that they hadn't decided as a couple, but she wasn't. It'd been so long since she'd gone anywhere, she really didn't care.

"Yes."

"Where? What do I need to bring? Will it be warm? Oh, I do love the beach and—"

"We won't be traveling."

"Oh." That was disappointing.

"You will need a dress for both Friday and Saturday night. Maybe even a different one for Saturday during the day."

"A dress? Where are we going that I have to wear a dress? I don't wear dresses. I don't own dresses." She preferred casual clothes, comfortable clothes.

CHAPTER 32: Harker

"You have the one you wore last night." He'd had vivid, hot dreams of that dress.

"My wedding dress?"

"Yes. It's not a traditional wedding dress with a long train and lace." It was slinky and sexy and perfect. "You don't need to wear the veil." He'd get her a blindfold. That was much better than a veil.

"Where are we going that you want me to wear my wedding dress?" She no longer sounded excited.

"I want you to keep an open mind." He'd lead her away from the uptight, Puritan beliefs of her childhood by appealing to her sense of adventure.

"You're making me nervous."

"Don't be. It's a reputable place. Nice people."

"Harker. Tell me where we're going."

"La Petite Mort Club."

"The sex club?"

Time to sooth her sensibilities and coax her into going. "Yes, but they have a fabulous restaurant, and the people are very nice. Everyone is polite, intelligent, excellent conversationalists and–"

"Do you know how hard it is to get in that place?" She almost vibrated off her chair. "I've wanted to go there for so long."

"You have?" Once again, she did what no one else ever could; she surprised him.

"Yes. I've never been to one. Do the people have sex right in the open? Have you ever seen someone tied up? Spanked? Flogged?" Her eyes got wider with each word.

"Yes. To all of those things."

"Oh...I can't wait."

"Me either." His innocent wife had a kinky streak that he couldn't wait to explore.

"But I'm not wearing my wedding dress."

"Why not?"

"I'll stand out."

"How do you know? You've never been there. Maybe white wedding dresses are normal attire."

"I've never been to Alaska either, but I know people don't walk around in bikinis."

"What does that have..." He stopped himself. He was not starting down that rabbit hole. They'd be arguing for the next few hours about typical attire for every freaking country in the world if he did. "Okay, most people don't wear white dresses at the Club, but I want you to wear it." People should notice her. She was different. Unique. Exceptional and he wanted everyone to see that she belonged to him.

"Too bad."

His jaw clenched. He could not punish her for this. She wasn't his submissive, at least not yet.

"I'll wear my black slacks with—"

"No. You don't have to wear your wedding dress, even though it'd make me happy, but I insist that you wear a dress or skirt." He needed easy access to her pussy.

"Do all the women at the Club wear dresses or skirts?"

"All of my women do." He cringed as soon as the words left his mouth. He knew better than to talk about other women in front of the current one.

"Well, I'm not. I honestly don't own any dresses. I never wear them."

"Then buy some." His comment about other women hadn't fazed her. That's right. Why would it? He wasn't a man she wanted to fuck.

"No." She wrinkled her nose. "I don't want to wear a dress or skirt."

"Then we aren't going." He'd teach her to obey. He'd prefer to paddle her lush, round ass but withholding pleasure would work too.

"Seriously? You won't take me there if I don't wear a dress." She sounded as disgusted as he felt.

"Yes." He waited for her to agree to his demands. She was used to this role. He was her boss. His word was final.

"You are such a...Fine. I'll buy a skirt."

"Three unless you want to wear the same one all weekend."

"Okay, but then you need to wear jeans."

"You don't get to tell me what to wear." That wasn't how this worked.

"Then I'm not going." She crossed her arms over her chest, challenging him with a look.

He'd call her bluff if he didn't want to fuck her so badly. Ethan was right. The Club was the perfect place to put her libido into overdrive. "I don't own jeans."

"I guess we can go shopping together."

"You will pay for this."

"Oh, no." She grabbed another pastry puff from the plate. "We're married. This is coming out of your account."

"That's not what I meant."

"I know." She grinned. "You'll try to get me back somehow, but you shouldn't have warned me. You know that saying. Forewarned is forearmed."

He nodded. She had no idea the kind of payment disobedience to him required, but he'd teach her and enjoy every torturously pleasurable moment.

CHAPTER 33: Harker

Harker closed his computer and stood, stretching. He was exhausted. After he and Alison had finished eating, they'd both gone back to work. It was well past midnight.

He left the room and headed down the hallway toward his bedroom. It was going to seem like forever before the weekend arrived. The best thing he could do was pretend like it was a month ago. He'd lived almost a year lusting after her in secret, he could handle a few more days. He just had to forget that she was his bride and she now belonged to him. Mind over matter. Stick to his routine. He flipped on his bedroom light. "Son of a bitch."

Alison was sleeping in his bed as if she belonged there. She did belong there. She was his wife. He had the right to crawl into bed and wake her with kisses on her neck, her lips, her breasts, across her abdomen and down to the juncture between her legs. She'd be wet for him and aching. He'd kiss her pussy, her moans of pleasure urging him on.

His dick which he'd bored into a coma with work, had perked up and was ready to play. He hadn't had sex in way too long. If Ethan hadn't interrupted him and Dahlia, he wouldn't be so fucking hard right now at the sight of a woman covered in a mound of blankets, but she wasn't some woman. She was his wife, and he hadn't touched her yet...because she didn't want him.

She rolled over, blinking as she sat up. "What's wrong? Why are you standing there?"

"You're in my bed."

"Huh?"

"Why are you in my bed? You have a room."

"I thought...We're married and..." Her eyes filled with hurt as she turned to get out of bed. "Sorry. I'll go."

"Don't." He felt like a complete ass. "It's okay. I was just surprised."

"I should've asked. It's not like this is a real marriage." She stood.

His gaze ran down her body. She wore the least sexy outfit he'd ever seen. It looked like a child's pajamas. It was plaid and the bottoms were long and so baggy he couldn't even make out a hint of her ass. The top was no better. It was buttoned up to her neck. She certainly hadn't worn this to entice him and yet, he was enticed. He wanted to unbutton her top, kissing ever bit of skin he revealed, tasting it with his tongue and lips until she writhed beneath him.

"I thought we'd share a bed. My parents did but I get it. We'll only be together when we...you know." She walked toward him, her eyes still sad.

He should tell her it was okay and that she could stay in his bed. The problem with that was he wouldn't last a night let alone a week without touching her. He couldn't risk it. If she laughed again, he didn't think he'd survive. So instead, he said, "It's best this way."

"Yeah. Good night." She smiled as she walked past him, but her lips trembled, and her lashes were damp from blinking away her tears.

It took everything he had not to call her back, but instead he closed the door, stripped and dropped onto his bed, shutting his eyes and grabbing his dick as he imagined peeling her out of those awful pajamas.

CHAPTER 34: Harker

Harker had thought he'd been in hell all week knowing Alison was his wife and not being able to touch her but that was just a prelude. This. This was hell. He glanced at his watch. They'd been at the mall for over three hours. Three Hours! And she still hadn't found even one dress or skirt. He'd bought his jeans in under twenty minutes. "Just pick a skirt and let's go eat."

"I have to find something that looks good. Slimming." She held the skirt up to her body. "And you're no help."

"What did I do? I told you I liked the gray one."

"The gray one made my butt look huge." She glanced over her shoulder, frowning at the lush, soft ass he'd been fantasizing about for months.

He'd imagined all sorts of activities with that butt—slapping it, kissing it, bending her over and watching his dick slide between those perfect round globes. "Well, I liked it." Not that it mattered what he liked but it should. His opinion should be the only one that mattered to her.

"You have no taste."

"I have taste." In his dreams he'd tasted her–over and over again, night after night.

It was Thursday evening and he'd had little to no sleep since Sunday. Every day, he'd worked until he couldn't keep his eyes open but once he dropped onto his bed, his exhaustion was replaced by lust. He could still smell the faint scent of her shampoo and perfume in his bed.

His mind would wander, imagining her in those baggy plaid pajamas sleeping so innocently down the hall from him. What would she do if he crept into her room and began to kiss her? He'd start at her feet and kiss his way up her body. He'd slide those giant pajama bottoms off and bury his face between her thighs. She'd taste so sweet as she wiggled and moaned, finally waking. Her eyes would flutter open and meet his. That's when his masturbatory fantasy turned into a dick destroying nightmare. Recognition would flare in her sleepy eyes right before she'd burst out laughing and every night his dick sagged in his hand.

He'd tried everything to find his release—remembering past lovers, imagining new lovers but nothing worked. His mind always went back to Alison in those ugly plaid pajamas.

"Don't worry." Alison patted his shoulder like he was some old man or small boy. "Your rescue is here." She waved at someone behind him.

He turned as Ellie walked toward them.

"Sorry I'm late. I just got out of work." Ellie hugged Alison and then smiled at him. "Harker."

"Ellie." Usually, he liked Alison's friend but today he loved her. "Is it really okay if I go? Seriously, you won't be mad?" He knew women and this seemed like a trap.

"Please. Go." Alison shoved him. "You weren't any help anyway."

"Thank God." He turned, ready to run for the door but stopped. "Ellie, she's to buy skirts or dresses. Don't let her get pants, slacks, shorts, jeans, capris, or anything else that isn't a skirt or dress."

"What about a kilt? May I buy one of those?" Alison asked sarcastically.

His mind shot back to those plaid pajamas and his voice was huskier than he would've liked when he said, "Yeah, a kilt will be fine."

"They don't wear anything under a kilt, do they?" asked Ellie.

"Then a kilt would be perfect." His eyes raked over Alison. Her cheeks flushed and he grinned. That was the first reaction she'd given him that made him think she was starting to see him as a fuckable man.

CHAPTER 35: Alison

"You have got to help me." Alison begged Ellie. "I hate skirts and dresses. They always make my ass look huge and that makes my breasts look even smaller."

"I'm glad to see you've changed your mind about Harker." Ellie grabbed Alison's hand and led her out of that store and toward a different one.

"Changed my mind? What are you talking about?"

"You want to look nice for him." Ellie smiled. "I get it but trust me, I think Harker likes how you look."

"Hardly." Alison's spirits, already low from not finding anything that didn't make her look like a pear, just became subterranean.

"Why do you think that and don't take how eager he was to get out of here as an indication. Men, especially ones like him, hate to shop."

"Even I know that." She truly wasn't offended that he'd practically charged out of the store like it was on fire. "I only brought him because I made him buy two pairs of jeans."

"You said he never wears jeans."

"He doesn't but if he wants me to wear a skirt or dress then he has to wear jeans."

"And he agreed?" Ellie stopped in the middle of the mall walkway.

"Yeah. Why are you smiling?" Her friend had a stupid look on her face.

"I told you he likes you." Ellie slapped Alison's shoulder.

"And I told you he doesn't. Not like that. Trust me." She tried not to let the hurt show, but they'd known each other a long time.

"What's wrong?" Ellie shifted direction and pulled her off to the side where there were less people.

"I'm not going to find a skirt standing in the corner." She didn't want to talk to anyone about this, least of all Ellie who'd never met a guy who hadn't wanted her.

"No, but we can talk. What's going on?"

Her friend wouldn't stop pestering until she told her so she may as well get it over with. "We haven't had sex yet. He doesn't want to, and I don't even sleep with him." She looked up, blinking furiously to keep from crying. "I really messed it all up on our wedding night. He was ready to do it and now he has no interest and...and I don't know why he doesn't want to do in vitro and it's a nightmare living with him. He's so grumpy and we barely talk at work anymore and after work is even worse and—"

"Okay. Okay." Ellie hugged her and then took her hands in hers. "Now, slow down. One thing at a time, okay?"

Alison nodded, wiping her eyes. She didn't even apologize for rambling because Ellie understood that was just how she talked.

"Did you tell him that you wanted to have sex?"

"Yes," she almost wailed.

"And he didn't?" Ellie looked confused. "That doesn't make any sense."

"It does when he can't...He isn't attracted to me."

"Oh honey, that is so not true."

"It is. He told me."

"He said he wasn't attracted to you?"

"Yes. I said we should, you know, and he said he didn't want to. That he...he had to...to"—thinking about it hurt enough, but saying it was like eating fire—"work himself up to...you know."

"What an ass." Ellie frowned but then shook her head. "It doesn't make sense. I see how he looks at you."

"You're confusing anger with lust."

"No, I'm not." Ellie pursed her lips. "You said he still doesn't want in vitro, right?"

"No. I offered and...and he was so mad—"

"You offered after he said he didn't want to have sex and he got mad at you for suggesting it?"

"Yes. I didn't suggest it right then. I couldn't. I had to get away from him, but later we were talking about how to fix this...this mess of a marriage. We both had ideas and I thought they were the same, but they weren't, and he got mad when I said in vitro."

"Did he tell you his plan to fix your marriage?"

"Yeah. That's why I need a skirt."

"Wearing a skirt will fix your marriage?" Ellie looked at her as if she had sprouted another head that was talking as much as her first one.

"No. Not exactly. He suggested a honeymoon and he wants me...insists that I wear a dress or skirt."

"Oh, he wants a honeymoon." Ellie grinned. "See. I told you he likes you."

"It's his way of working up"—she waved her hand in front of her thighs—"his attraction. He must have a thing for skirts or something. Maybe he's a leg man but my legs aren't that great. My thighs are too heavy from sitting all day. I should exercise but—"

"Your legs are perfect but where are you going for your honeymoon?"

"Oh, he's taking me to La Petite Mort Club for the weekend." She grinned. "I've always wanted to go there. I never told him that. I don't know how he knew—"

"He's taking you to La Petite Mort Club?"

"Yeah. Isn't it exciting? Now I can stop pestering you to get me in there."

"Oh, Alison. We have to find you the perfect outfit and sexy underwear because that man definitely wants you...a lot." Ellie grabbed her hand and dragged her across the mall to the lingerie shop.

CHAPTER 36: Alison

"I can't believe I'm actually here." Alison turned to Harker as he pulled the car into the parking garage at La Petite Mort Club. "What's it like inside? Is everyone hot and sexy? Will they be doing it right at the door? Are there beds or do people do it on chairs or standing or—"

"You'll see." He parked and got out.

Alison hurried out of the car, her loose, black skirt falling back into place without any tugging from her. She'd been surprised but happy when Ellie had suggested a loose skirt instead of one that clung to her curves like a second skin. She actually felt like she looked good in this outfit.

Her skirt fell to mid-thigh with a small slit up the back. It was simple with straight lines and as far as skirts went it was okay, but she loved her new shirt. It was soft peach that made her brown eyes look like caramelly-chocolate, but the best part was it actually made her breasts look good.

"This way." Harker started for the door.

"Wait. Our bags." She stood by the trunk. She didn't want any excuse for them to leave. She'd waited too long to get inside this place.

"I'll send someone to get them."

"You sure? We could get them now and put them in the room."

"Or you can trust me. They'll get to our room before we do."

"This isn't some trick to shorten the trip if you get mad at me again, is it?" She eyed him warily. "Because you said we were staying until Sunday. You can leave if you want to but I'm staying here until Sunday."

He took two large steps and stopped so close his chest almost brushed against hers. She had to tip back her head to see his face.

"Three things. First, this isn't a trick. Second, don't do anything to piss me off and third, if I leave you will be coming with me."

"No, I won't."

"You're not staying alone." His jaw tightened.

"Then I guess you'd better not get mad at me because if you want to leave early, you'll have to drag me out of here." She stepped around him and started in the direction he'd been walking.

He caught up to her quickly, grabbing her arm and yanking her to his side. "Don't tempt me because I will do exactly that."

"You would not." She laughed. She couldn't even picture it. "You'd never do anything so...so—"

"Passionate?" He studied her face.

"No." She laughed again. "Undignified. And it would be undignified because I'd be kicking and screaming." She grinned up at him. "We'd make a scene, and you wouldn't like that at all." He was the most reserved man she'd ever met.

He captured her chin. "Me tossing you over my shoulder and carrying you away–no matter how much you fought–wouldn't even come close to qualifying as a scene at the Club."

"Really? Then what does?" Oh, she couldn't wait to get inside.

"You'll see if you ever stop arguing with me."

"I wasn't arguing. I was explaining that I'm not leaving until Sunday. I don't care what happens."

"Speaking of that"—his thumb caressed her cheek—"you need to pick a safeword."

"A safeword? Why? Are we going to..."? She didn't even know what to call it. Suddenly, he seemed so big and masculine, his hand large and his fingers rough on her face.

"It's always good to be prepared."

"True and I've been thinking about this and—"

"You have?" He seemed surprised.

"Yep. For years."

"Really?" His eyes darkened and his lips shifted upward in a half-smile.

She nodded. "Ever since I heard about the place."

"Okay, then what's your safeword?"

"Debug."

"Debug?"

"Yeah. From what I've read a person uses a safeword if they want things to stop...even if only for a moment. When I have a bug in my code it forces me to stop and fix it. I figured it's kind of the same thing. Right?"

"Actually, yes. It's perfect"—he moved a little closer and she suddenly didn't have enough air—"because if you use your safeword I'll stop but only long enough to fix it."

CHAPTER 37: Harker

Harker led Alison into the bar. "Are you sure you don't want to get some dinner? The food here is excellent."

"No." She sat at the bar, her head almost spinning as she tried to take everything in at once. "This place is beautiful."

"It is nice." He sat next to her.

The Club was elegant but understated. The lighting was subtle, just enough to add mystery. The bar was solid wood with etchings of couples participating in various adult activities along the sides, the couches and chair were upholstered in different shades, some blended into the background while others added a splash of color.

"Why don't I order something for you to snack on." He didn't want a repeat of their wedding night.

"Oh. I'm sorry." The excitement in her eyes changed to concern. "I didn't even think. You're hungry. Let's go to the restaurant." She started to stand.

"Sit." He touched her arm. Her thought and consideration for others always amazed him. He was pretty sure she'd literally give someone the shirt off her back. His eyes darted to her chest. He wouldn't mind seeing that. Maybe he should say he was cold.

"No, let's go eat. I can look around later. I don't want you to get grumpy.

"I don't get grumpy. I'm not a child."

"Ha. You're always grumpy but you're way worse when you're hungry."

"I'm not hungry." He tugged on her hand. "Now, sit down."

"Are you sure? I don't mind going to the restaurant."

The bartender stopped in front of them. "Hey Harker. Miss."

"Bea, this is Alison. Alison, this is Bea, the best bartender here." He'd spent many nights talking with Bea and some of the regulars.

"Nice to meet you." Alison leaned forward, her eyes dancing with curiosity. "What's it like working here? I bet you have a ton of stories." She glanced around. "Is everyone that comes here so...so...perfect. I didn't think people like this existed outside of the movies. Or I guess Hollywood because they are real people. Most of us...."

Alison continued to ramble, and Bea glanced at him with an amused expression on her face.

He shrugged. "She's excited to be here. Bring her a glass of zinfandel and I'll have a bourbon on the rocks."

"Got it." Bea patted Alison's hand. "It's a great place to work. You should talk to Ethan about a job if you're interested. He's always looking for new Pleasure Associates."

"Really?" She sounded flattered. "Do you think he'd hire me?"

"No. Absolutely not." He was not letting her work here.

The two women frowned at him and Alison's big, brown eyes filled with hurt.

"What did I say?"

"Don't listen to him." Bea gave him a disgusted look. "I know Ethan a lot better than Harker and he'd hire you in a heartbeat."

"Oh...shit. No, I didn't mean he wouldn't hire you." He'd fucked that one up big time. "I meant there is no way in hell I'm letting you work here."

"Oh." The hurt fled from Alison's gaze and she grinned but it quickly turned into a frown. "Letting me?"

"Yes. Letting you." He was her husband, damn it.

"Oh. I get it." She had this ability to work everything out in her head to her satisfaction, but she often had it all wrong. "Don't worry. I'd still work for you, but I could work here part-time."

"Ethan hires part-time," said Bea. "You won't get benefits but—"

"I said no." His wife wasn't going to moonlight as a Pleasure Associate. "Why don't you get our drinks?"

"Got it." Bea smirked at him as she walked away.

"Harker, you can't tell me what I can do."

Oh, he could, and he would. However, saying that right now wasn't a good idea. He didn't need to fight, especially not tonight. "You won't have time between working for me and caring for our child."

"Oh yeah. That." Her smiled faded.

"Yeah, that." He couldn't wait to have a kid, to make a child with her and she was dreading every moment.

Bea dropped off their drinks and went to wait on another customer.

"What's going on." Alison's gaze brightened again as she stared across the room. "Looks like people are moving toward that stage. Is there going to be a show?" She turned toward him, not even realizing that she'd pissed him off. "Do you think someone is going to have sex up there?"

"Of course, they are," he snapped. He may as well be the bar stool for as much attention as she paid him. "This is a sex club."

"Who is that guy? Do you know him? He's gorgeous." She literally fanned herself and then her hand clasped onto his forearm. "He's taking off his shirt."

"Yes, I know him." Suddenly he wasn't so sure about Ethan's plan.

Anthony was a very good-looking man. Women found Harker attractive mostly because of his wealth and power but they melted at Anthony's feet just like they did Ethan's.

"What's he like? Is he nice? Mean? Oh..." Her hand tightened on his arm so much he wouldn't be surprised to find nail marks on his skin. "What's he doing? Is that a paddle? What's he going to do to her?"

Good plan or bad, that was his cue. "Do you want to move closer and see?" He wasn't thrilled that her pussy was dripping for Anthony but right now, he'd take her and her wet pussy any way he could get them.

"Can we?" Her eyes sparkled with excitement like a kid with a credit card in a toy store.

"Absolutely." He stood, holding out his hand.

She didn't even hesitate, sliding her small hand into his as she stood.

"Take your drink. You may need it."

"Oh, right." She grabbed her wine. "Are you going to take yours?"

"No." He tossed it back in two gulps.

"Are you ordering another one?"

"No."

"Then why—"

"I want my hands free."

"Why?" Her nose wrinkled as she tried to figure it out in her head.

He bit back a curse. Any other woman would know exactly why her date...her husband wanted his hands free but to Alison, he wasn't a man. That was going to change very soon because if it didn't, he'd probably drop to his knees and whimper at her feet. "Think about it. Why do you think I'd want my hands free?"

"Is this interactive?" Her eyes darted to the stage. "Are we supposed to help...to participate?"

"Of course not." He glared at her. She wasn't going to see him as a man until he fucked her.

"Well, excuse me. You don't have to get so snotty. I've never been to a place like this."

"You're right." Anger wasn't the key to getting him laid. He calmed his temper. "Let me assure you that Anthony doesn't require any assistance."

"Have you...Have you ever done that...on stage?"

"Yes. Would you like to get on stage?" He moved closer to her. "Be tied up. Vulnerable. While everyone watched."

"No." The word came out breathless.

"I think you would." He captured her chin, caressing her soft skin.

"No," she repeated.

"Your eyes say yes." They were alight with anticipation and excitement.

"They...they lie. I could never do that."

"You could. I can show you." His thumb slid over her lower lip and she opened her mouth slightly. It was the only invitation he needed, probably the only one he was going to get. "You can trust me." He dipped his head, moving toward her mouth.

CHAPTER 38: Alison

Alison's heart thudded fast and irregular as Harker leaned toward her. He was going to kiss her. Harker. Now. A kiss. She'd never realized how big and how male he was. His lips were firm but full, his face narrow–the hint of his beard beginning to show on his cheeks. His breath tickled her lips. The scent was a mix between smoky bourbon and mint from his toothpaste. Her body drifted toward him, her eyes closing. She wanted to taste that smell.

"I promise. I'll never hurt you. I'll only show you pleasure beyond anything you've ever imagined." He shifted, whispering in her ear. "Come. Before we miss the show."

Her eyes opened as he stepped away from her, taking her hand in his and leading her across the room. He hadn't kissed her. He'd been going to. Why had he stopped? Was her breath bad? She'd brushed her teeth right before they'd left the house. She'd check by cupping her hand over her mouth, but he had one hand and her other held her glass. She downed her drink and sidestepped to place it on a nearby table.

"What are you do...You finished your drink already?" He wasn't pleased.

"Ah...yeah. I was thirsty."

"You aren't getting another one for a while. I don't want you shitfaced again."

"Don't worry. I don't want another one." She frowned at him. "But if I did, I'd get one."

"No. You wouldn't." His hand tightened on hers as he pulled her into the crowd that'd gathered to watch Anthony. He stopped, stepping behind her. "Can you see the stage from here?"

"Yeah." She'd argue about the drink, but she didn't want one and she didn't want to miss the show.

The man Harker had called Anthony walked around a petite, skinny woman with breasts that had to be fake because they were huge, and she was so tiny.

"How does she even stay upright with those things?"

"What?" Harker leaned closer, his lips by her ear. "I didn't hear you."

"Nothing." She grimaced. She hadn't meant to say that out loud. The woman on stage had black hair and pale features. She was very pretty, but a guy who looked like Anthony wouldn't be with someone ugly. Nothing was happening. Anthony just walked around the woman. She glanced behind her at Harker. "What's he doing?"

"He's making her wait." He stared at the stage. "Making her understand that he's the boss. He'll give her a command in a minute or two. As soon as he's ready."

Ellie was right. Harker was a good-looking guy–harsh features that made him seem unapproachable, strong and so sexy. She'd known this. She'd just forgotten, or she'd pushed it out of her mind because a man like him would never want a plain woman like her...except he did. It was only for her genes, but her body would get to participate if he could muster up enough desire to do the deed. Was that why he hadn't kissed her? She cupped her hand over her mouth, breathed out and sniffed. Her breath was fine. That meant it was the rest...

"What are you doing?" He stared down at her.

"Nothing." Her cheeks heated as she quickly looked back at the stage and her mouth dropped open.

Anthony stood in front of the woman as she unbuttoned her shirt. Alison wasn't into women, but she couldn't look away as the woman on stage stripped. She seemed oblivious to everyone but Anthony. It was as if no one else in the world mattered or even existed. The man held out his hand and the woman gave him her shirt. He folded it and placed it neatly on a chair on the stage. The woman started to undo her skirt, but Anthony said something before glancing into the crowd. Alison's breath caught. She swore he stared right at her. She stumbled backward, bumping into Harker's strong frame. His hands, large and hot, captured her hips, steadying her.

The woman handed Anthony her bra and he placed that on the chair too.

"Why is he putting her clothes on that chair?" In her experience clothes were tossed aside to be gathered later.

"He's taking care of her." Harker leaned down, his words a hot whisper in her ear. "She belongs to him. Her comfort, her pleasure is his responsibility"—his fingers danced along her cheek, pushing her hair aside—"to give or to withhold."

She shivered as his lips teased her ear and she turned toward him, her heart racing when he captured her chin. He was finally going to kiss her. She'd never wanted anything as much as this. His breath teased across her lips. His mouth was so close that if she stood on tiptoes their lips would touch.

"Watch the stage." He turned her face away from his and she almost screamed in frustration.

CHAPTER 39: Harker

Harker grinned over the top of Alison's head. She'd been soft and willing, her body leaning into his as he'd whispered in her ear. Then she'd turned, her lips open, wanting...no, expecting his kiss. She'd been so surprised when he hadn't kissed her...again. Women were so used to getting everything they wanted sexually from men that it drove them mad when they were denied. It made them desperate for that man's touch, his kiss and his cock. That was exactly how he needed Alison tonight–desperate for him.

He shifted closer, making sure to keep his dick away from her. She wasn't ready to feel that pressed against her ass, but soon. He stared at the stage. The sub was tied to a spanking bench, her ass in the air but still covered by her skirt. That was Anthony's gift to him so Harker could play along with the scene. He'd have to thank Ethan for arranging this.

"What do you think that woman is feeling?" he whispered in her ear. "She's tied up. Helpless. At the mercy of her dom."

"I...I don't know." Alison's breath came faster with each word.

"Do you think she's nervous?" His hand drifted just a little under her shirt right above the waistband of her skirt. "Is she eager?" Her skin was so soft and warm. "Is her breath coming faster? Is her heart racing, waiting for him to kiss her, touch her?" His hand slid upward. He wanted to grab it and tease her nipple until she screamed but not yet. His fingers traced gently between her breasts. "Do you think her heart is beating like yours? Fast. Unsteady." He nipped her ear. "Answer me."

CHAPTER 40: Alison

"Yes." Alison couldn't think straight with Harker's hand between her breasts, but she also couldn't pull her eyes away from the stage.

The woman was tied to that bench, helpless and exposed as Anthony stood behind her, his hands running up and down her legs, over her ass and across her sides as he checked the restraints. Alison's nipples tightened, her lacy bra scratchy against her sensitive nubs as the man's fingers teased the woman's breasts. Alison's back arched in a silent plea for Harker to touch her breasts, tease her nipples.

"Is she eager for him?" His deep voice slipped inside her head, whispering all her secret thoughts of desire. "For his kiss?"

She wanted his kiss on her neck, her lips, her breasts. Everywhere. She leaned against him, enveloped in his warmth and scent. His hand moved down to her waist and his fingers caressed the skin of her belly. Her body tightened, wanting those fingers to move lower, to touch her where she throbbed.

"Answer me. Do you think she's eager?" His words were rough and thick in her ear.

"Yes." Her voice was soft and yet filled with need as the man on stage teased the woman with his touch. His hand skimming up her legs, barely sliding under the hem of the woman's skirt. "Why isn't he...doing something?" She leaned more heavily against Harker. Why wasn't Harker doing something was the real question.

"Watch." He kissed her ear. "He will."

"I've never seen anyone...you know...have sex. I've seen pornos but nothing in real life. I...I don't know what I'll think. Sex isn't actually too pretty. I mean it's great when you're doing it but watching is...I like the foreplay and all...but the act itself is kind of...I don't know."

"I think you'll enjoy it. Anthony knows how to put on a show."

"Oh...shoot. I hadn't realized I'd said that all out loud." She shifted to see his face. She so often said things that annoyed or disgusted people.

"Don't apologize. I love your frankness." His dark eyes sparkled. "I always know where I stand with you. I never have to try and figure out if you're mad at me."

"But you tell me to shut up."

"I don't say that." His brow creased.

She turned toward him, but he didn't move his arms and that meant he was holding her. It should be strange or amusing like the other night because this was Harker, but it felt right. "You say that to me all the time." She lowered her voice, mimicking him. "Alison, stop talking and let me think."

"That's not the same as shut up."

"Yes, it is."

"No, it isn't." He captured her chin, his thumb tracing over her lower lip. "I never want you to shut up...just pause for a moment." He lowered his face toward hers until his mouth was only a breath away. "Sometimes not talking is good."

She didn't think; her body just responded and she leaned into him. He wasn't Harker the barking boss. He was Harker the man and he was hers...at least for a bit.

His eyes darkened but he kissed her on the forehead and turned her around. "Watch the stage. The show's about to get good."

"Wha..." Her words died as the guy on stage stood next to the small table. "Is that a flogger? And"—she squinted—"a riding crop and...What are those gloves? They have spikes on them." Was this a sex show or a horror movie?

"Vampire gloves." He pulled her back to his chest.

"Vampire...Why are there spikes on them?"

The man on stage picked up the paddle he'd had earlier and walked over to the woman.

"Imagine them on your skin." Harker's voice teased her ear like the devil telling her about things she didn't know...things she shouldn't be curious about, but she was. "Think of how they'd feel caressing your legs, your breasts. The spikes sharp but his touch gentle...at first."

"At first?" Her body trembled.

"He might run them between your legs."

The man on stage stuck the paddle in the back of his pants and ran his hands up the woman's legs raising her skirt.

Harker's fingers teased along the back of her thigh where her skin met her skirt. "He'd be gentle. Teasing." His nails skimmed along her legs. "He'd move slowly, letting you feel every inch he touched, letting you imagine how it'll be when he runs those spikes gently where you ache." His hands moved upward, taking her skirt with them.

The cool air from the room did nothing to cool her passion as the man on stage exposed the woman's round ass. Anthony's fingers played between the woman's legs as Harker's hand pushed Alison's skirt up and over her ass. His body hid her backside, but the front of her skirt lifted too. Anyone who looked would see her red panties. She should tell him to stop, but nothing came out of her mouth but soft pants of anticipation. She wanted him to touch her like the man on stage was touching that woman.

Harker caressed the outside of her thigh, his fingers dancing along the soft skin. "Is her pulse pounding between her legs too? Is she needy and aching for his touch?" His hand trailed between her thighs. "He'll want to know that he pleases her." His voice was gruff, and his cock pushed against her ass. "He'll need to discover for himself if she's ready. Words can lie." He tightened his arm around her waist as his other hand teased along the front of her thighs.

The woman on stage moaned and Anthony stepped away from her and licked his fingers. Alison's body gushed and she squeezed her legs together.

"Are you wet?" He nibbled on her ear, his fingers circling as they slowly moved inward on her thigh, getting closer and closer to her core. "Women are so soft. So different from men." He kissed her neck, a whisper of a touch that felt like a jolt of lightning. She leaned harder against him. "You're so giving and open. You open everything for us." His fingers tickled across her pussy and her stance widened as if his touch were magic.

The man on stage held the paddle but Alison was so focused on the sensations that Harker was making in her body that nothing registered until she heard the slap ring out through the club.

"He hit her." Her body stiffened.

"Yes. He did." Harker's grip on her waist tightened, pulling her closer to him, his cock hard and long pressing against her ass.

"Why would..."

The man hit the woman again, the paddle leaving her butt a rosy shade of red.

"For pleasure."

"That doesn't seem..."

"Rough can be good." Harker's hand slid between her legs and cupped her pussy. "Very good."

She shivered as sparks seemed to fly from his fingers where they pressed against her. He rubbed hard and fast between her legs. Her wetness making the panties slide back and forth. Her hips rolled into his touch, pushing his hand harder against her aching flesh. She had to touch him. She reached up, her arms lifting over her head and clasping around his neck. He shoved her underwear aside, his fingers sliding between her slick folds and she moaned.

Anthony put the paddle down and knelt behind the woman, spreading her ass cheeks and burying his face between her legs. The woman's moan echoed through the room.

Harker's breath in her ear was ragged as he stroked between her legs, his thumb teasing her clit, pushing her closer and closer to orgasm.

He slid one long finger inside her and her body clenched onto him. He thrust another finger inside her, pumping faster and faster. Her stance widened as she clung to him, her hips wiggling.

"I need to taste you. Make you scream."

Oh god, she wanted him on his knees, his face buried between her legs like the man on stage. A low guttural moan slipped from her lips and a few people turned toward them.

"Harker. Stop. They're watching—"

"Ignore them." His voice was rough, commanding.

She wanted to but they were watching, and she couldn't do this. She pushed at his hand. "Harker, stop."

"No," he whispered in her ear.

CHAPTER 41: Harker

"Alison, if you want me to stop, use your safeword." Otherwise, Harker had no intention of stopping until he fucked her. He stepped in front of her and dropped to his knees, her body tightening around his fingers.

"Stop." Alison's eyes darted over his head.

They were starting to draw the attention of more people. Stop wasn't something that was said often at La Petite Mort Club. Red or yellow wouldn't have made anyone blink but stop was a newbie word and the patrons loved watching a novice learn.

"Look at me." He stared up at her and her eyes dropped to his. He pulled his fingers from her body and slid them into his mouth. She tasted delicious—sweet with a tang of tart, just like her personality.

Her breath hitched but then her eyes darted over his head and to the side. Her body stiffened with panic. He'd moved too fast. He tugged her skirt down and stood. Her gaze met his. It was calmer now but still a little wild.

He touched her cheek. "Next time use your safeword. It's the only way I know for sure you actually want to stop."

She nodded.

He pulled her in front of him again.

"Harker, I can't—"

"We'll just watch. I promise." He kissed her neck before resting his face against the side of her head and wrapping his arms around her waist. He wanted her to have his child. She fit perfectly in his business life, but he'd never planned on bringing her here, having her participate in this part of his life. Maybe for the time they were together they could have both.

"Okay." She relaxed against him, her hands on his forearms.

She'd be a challenging sub, but that'd make her surrender that much better. She already trusted him. They'd spent a lot of time together. Now he just had to convince her that he knew her body better than she did.

CHAPTER 42: Alison

Alison was horrified that she'd let Harker finger her while people watched. She'd been raised to believe that sex was a private affair between two married people.

Harker was sort of her husband, but they'd almost had sex in public. Not a quickie in a restaurant bathroom or in a dark movie theater but fooling around in a crowd of people who watched them openly. Her brain screamed, *what were you thinking?* While her body shouted, *why did you stop?*

Harker's body warmed her back, and his strong arms circled her waist. He wasn't doing anything sexual but everything about him was sensual—his strength, his warmth, his steady heartbeat and his dick, hard and long pressing against her bottom. She hadn't used her safeword because every thought in her head had fled in her panic and yet, he'd stopped. She felt safe and more turned on than she'd ever been.

On top of all of that she couldn't pull her eyes away from the stage where Anthony still worked his sub. He slapped her with the flogger, the long straps landing on the woman's back and ass. Her screams sharp and loud turned into moans of pleasure.

"Why does she like it? It has to hurt. Those red welts can't feel good."

"But they can," he whispered. "The pain takes you to another place. A place of nothing but feeling and sensation. A place just for the two of you."

"But..." She didn't get it.

"Do you like rough sex?" His voice had turned gravelly, and he pulled her back, pressing his cock more firmly against her ass.

"Sometimes," she whispered as if too afraid to admit it out loud, but her body wasn't afraid. It knew what it wanted, and her hips shifted, rubbing against him.

His breath hissed in her ear. "Just like that. Pain and pleasure together. Separate but one."

Anthony dropped the flogger and undid his pants.

"Holy shit. He's huge." Alison couldn't pull her eyes away from that man's dick.

"He is." There was a smile in Harker's tone.

"I mean...Wow." She'd never seen a man with a cock like that. It was thick and long. Huge in all ways. "Maybe that's why he flogged her. He had to get her ready for the real pain because there's no way that's going to feel good. He's too..."

Anthony began pushing into the woman. Her moan echoed through the Club, but it wasn't a sound of pain.

"I think she'd argue with you." Harker's hands slid under her blouse. He didn't move them toward her breasts or her pussy, but his touch on her bare skin made her body purr.

"She does seem to be enjoying it." Alison swallowed, lost in the intense pleasure on that woman's face. She wanted that. She needed that.

Anthony began to thrust slowly in and out. His hand wrapped in the woman's hair, pulling back her head and making her face even more visible. Her expression was exquisite—pleasure, pain, tension and release.

Alison's fingers wrapped around Harker's hands. She had to touch him. Anthony's pace increased and Alison's breath raced as she rubbed her ass against Harker's cock. She needed him between her legs, inside her body. She turned, wrapping her arms around his neck.

He stared down at her, his eyes as dark as a moonless night. "What do you want Alison?"

"Kiss me." This time she wasn't giving him the chance to move away or to kiss her cheek or forehead. She raised up onto her tiptoes and kissed him.

CHAPTER 43: Harker

As soon as Alison's lips touched his, Harker's control vanished. He'd wanted her for so fucking long. His hands slid under her skirt, cupping her ass and lifting her against him. His tongue slid across her lips. She opened immediately, letting him inside but it wasn't enough. A kiss would never be enough. He turned and headed for the back of the Club.

She pulled her mouth away from his. "Where are you going? Put me down."

"No." This time she'd have to say her safeword because otherwise nothing would stop him from fucking his wife.

"But..." She glanced around. "People are looking at us."

"So." He walked faster. No way in hell was he going to be forced to slow down because of the crowd again. "Your ass is covered. Most of it anyway." Her loose skirt hung over his hands.

"Yeah, but they're watching us."

"Again, so what?" He kissed her. It was hard and fast, taking her breath away and making his speed up. "You need to pay attention to me. Not them."

"Do I?" Her eyes sparkled with humor. "This is familiar."

"How's that?" He turned down a hallway.

"It's what you're like at work."

"I've never said that to you at work."

"Not in those exact words but you do say it." She used her Harker voice which he hated. "Alison, come here. Alison, where are you? Alison, why is my computer not working?"

He shifted, pulling the keycard for their room from his pocket as he stopped at the door.

"Alison, I need you," she continued. "Alison, get in here."

"Alison, get in here." He opened the door and stepped inside, kicking it shut behind him. He loosened his hold on her ass and let her slide down his body. "Alison, I need you."

CHAPTER 44: Alison

Alison's stupid heart melted at Harker's words and the intensity in his eyes. It was like he meant it, like this was real and not some pretend marriage where he had to work up his attraction to her. But she refused to think about that because right now, he did desire her. His proof had been poking her ass all night. It didn't matter if he didn't want her forever. She didn't want him forever either, but she did want him right now.

She grabbed his shirt and pulled him to her, running the tip of her tongue along his lips and then sliding inside when he opened. He groaned into her mouth and shoved her against the door. She swore he must've grown three more hands because he touched her everywhere, squeezing her breasts, grabbing her ass, cupping her chin and tipping her head as he deepened the kiss.

His mouth devoured hers, his tongue thrusting inside as he pressed her against the door, his body large and strong pushing into her softness. It'd been so long since she'd kissed a man, had a man want her. Her hands tangled in his hair. It was thick and soft, unlike the rest of him that was so very hard. Her legs opened as he moved between them, his cock rubbing against her and she moaned into his mouth.

He grasped her hair, pulling back her head as his mouth moved off hers a fraction. His warm breath teased her lips. She fell into his dark gaze as he pushed up her shirt. She lifted her arms and he yanked it over her head, tossing it aside.

"Aren't you going to fold it like Anthony did?" she teased.

"Are you agreeing to be my sub?" His fingers slid up her torso and unhooked the clasp at the front of her bra.

"Your...sub? You mean doing everything you say. Kissing your ass to keep you happy. I thought I did all that as your employee."

"You do." His lips quirked in a half-smile. "But as my sub it's not my ass you'll be kissing." He slid the bra from her arms, his dark eyes almost glowing as he stared at her chest.

Her breasts were small but the way he looked at her made her feel, for the first time in her life, like she wasn't lacking in the boob department. She reached between them and stroked him through his pants. "What would you like me to..."

His mouth came down on her breast, fast and hard, sucking and teasing her with his tongue. Sensation shot from her nipple to her pussy, making it clench and throb.

"Oh..." Her hands went back to his hair, holding him closer as he kissed his way to her other breast. His hand drifted between her legs, his long fingers stroking her pussy in featherlight touches. She rocked against him, trying to make him touch her harder.

His teeth grazed her nipple, tugging gently. Her body tensed and melted at the same time and then he bit down.

"Ouch...ohhh..." The sting shot straight between her legs, throbbing and dark.

"And now." He lifted his head, his eyes gleaming as he kissed her quickly. "I'm going to do that to your pussy."

"Hark..." But he was already on his knees.

He shoved her skirt up and yanked her underwear down, lifting her feet, one at a time to get the panties out of his way. He grasped her thighs, pulling her legs apart, his hot breath whispering across her swollen flesh. He spread her lower lips with his thumbs and blew on her slick folds, teasing her. He looked up at her. "Is this funny?"

"What?" She almost panted. She needed his mouth on her.

"Do you find this funny?"

"No." What was he talking about? Was this some weird kink? "Why?"

He raised one brow at her.

"Oh. That." Damn him. Would he never get over that? She'd die...right after she killed him...if this was his way of getting back at her for their wedding night. "I apolo..."

"Good because I don't find it funny either. I find it delicious." His hot tongue licked along her seam, before swirling around her clit and she almost melted into a puddle of passion.

CHAPTER 45: Harker

Harker tried to be gentle, but he'd waited too long to touch Alison and he'd make sure she never laughed at the thought of him going down on her again—ever.

She was pink and wet, swollen and glistening for him. Him. He'd done this to her, no one else. He breathed her in, his cock pressing against his pants, but he wasn't rushing this. He leaned in, licking up and down her center. She was hot and delicious. He alternated his stroke between just the tip and burying his face against her and using his entire tongue. Her fingers tightened in his hair, pulling him closer to her pussy. Her sexy mews of pleasure made his cock rock hard. He'd done the impossible. He'd rendered her speechless. He shoved his tongue inside her, licking deep. She tugged on his hair as her legs trembled and her hips began to thrust against his face. She was close but there was no way he was letting her come without his dick buried deep inside her. He undid his pants and stood, shoving them out of his way.

Her eyes were half-closed and so dark, her lips open and wet. He had to have her now. He grabbed his cock, sliding it along her hot, wet seam. He rested his head on her forehead, his breath mixing with hers as he pushed the tip inside her. She was so hot and tight, squeezing his dick as he slid inside a little more.

She moaned softly, her hands slipping to his shoulders, her nails scraping along his skin. He couldn't wait. He had to make her his. He shoved inside her all the way. His cock growing even longer at her sharp intake of breath. Fuck yeah. He was a man. A fuckable one and she knew it.

He pulled out and slid slowly back inside. She was perfect. Made for him. His body screamed for him to pump into her, to fuck her fast and hard but by her tightness and shallow breathing she wasn't ready for that. His chest heaved as he slowed down. He had to wait. To make it good for her. He planned on doing this again—every day at least two or three times a day—and that meant he'd better make it really good for her.

CHAPTER 46: Alison

Alison's breath hitched and her heart raced. Harker was big and it'd been so long since she'd had sex that she felt every inch of him as he stretched her. It was a little painful, but it also felt so good as he touched those places that ached for his heat and hardness.

He kissed her softly, his large hands gently cupping her face. It was sweet but she didn't want sweet. Sweet was for later. She wanted sex—hot, hard fucking—just like she'd seen on stage. She kissed him back, her tongue sliding inside his mouth. His tongue tangled with hers, his body pressing harder against her. She sucked, pulling him deeper inside her mouth. His fingers tightened on her face as his hips moved, pumping into her hard and fast.

She groaned and he stopped, staring into her eyes. He didn't say anything, but she could see the question. "Yes."

He caressed her cheek, his gaze still unsure.

"Please, Harker. I need you." She'd never in her life imagined she'd say those words but somehow, right now, they felt right.

"Fuck." He pulled her arms over her head, his body rocking into hers—in and out, over and over. He bent, his mouth capturing her nipple and sucking as he fucked her harder and faster.

He was big and although she was wet and ready every thrust stung a little before it shifted and twisted into pleasure. She needed to be closer. She lifted her legs, wrapping them around his thighs. The movement made his dick shift inside her and she moaned. The sound spurred him on, and his thrusts became shorter and harder, sparking a flame so hot and so deep she burned from the inside out. Her skin flushed as her hips rocked with his thrusts. She clawed at his back, his muscles working under her fingertips and making her even wetter. His hand tangled in her hair again, pulling back her head as he kissed her, biting her lip as his other hand slid between her legs and stroked her clit. Sensation shot through her and she shattered, clinging to him.

CHAPTER 47: Harker

Alison's little sounds of pleasure as she came almost sent Harker over the edge, but he wasn't done yet. He thrust into her, slow and steady, riding out her orgasm. His thumb circled her clit and he tugged on her hair, making her focus on him. "Again."

Her eyes widened and she opened her mouth, but nothing came out. If he wasn't so close to busting his nuts he would've grinned. Again he'd made her speechless. He pulled almost all the way out and then pushed back inside her in one long thrust as his thumb pressed down on her clit.

She screamed, her body writhing under his, trying to escape but she belonged to him now. She was his to please and she wasn't getting away until he let her go. He pulled her legs from his hips, dropping one and lifting the other between them. He slid into her balls deep. Her body was tighter this way, and he gritted his teeth as tingles ran down his spine. He wasn't going to last long but he was going to make every second count. He rocked into her over and over, her body coming back to life with each thrust until she was clinging to his cock. Her nails dug into his shoulders as he fucked her faster and harder. He'd never been a gentle lover. Gentle was for women and sensitive guys. He fucked like a man—hot and hard and in control.

He lowered his face to her neck, inhaling her scent and then kissed her, tugging her skin into his mouth, and biting down as his dick pumped into her. Her body froze and then bucked almost violently, clinging to his cock, as she came. He grunted, his body heaving as he thrust into her over and over until he exploded, his dick emptying inside her.

CHAPTER 48: Alison

Alison rested her hand over Harker's heart. Last night had been wonderful. After their encounter at the door all she'd wanted was to fall asleep in his arms, but he'd had other plans.

He'd carried her to bed and had slowly removed the rest of her clothes. He'd taken his time, kissing every inch of her skin until she was panting and ready to toss him on his back and jump him, but this time he'd gone slow. Freaking unbelievably slow. She'd never been with a man who'd been able to withstand coming for more than a few minutes once he was inside her...but Harker had fucked her forever. He'd slid inside her and had pushed her to the edge over and over again. She'd come, screaming and panting and he'd slow down, switching positions and starting all over again. She'd lost track of everything in the storm of pleasure he'd created until she was nothing but a boneless pile of flesh.

She leaned up, staring down at him. He looked so sweet, his normal gruffness gone and his face relaxed. She ran her hand over his skin, loving the feel of his chest hair–softer than it looked, kind of like Harker. Her eyes drifted over his body. He was so damn sexy. How had she blocked that from her mind?

She knew why she'd done it. Self-preservation. She'd always been practical and a rich, sexy guy like him dated models, not plain geeks like her. It would hurt when this was over. He'd go back to his models and she'd go back to other geeks but until then, she'd enjoy him. He was a woman's fantasy come to life with broad shoulders that tapered to a lean waist and hips and a perfectly sized cock—not too big and definitely not too small. Her hand skimmed down his chest and she strummed her fingers over his abdomen.

She'd always enjoyed sex, but it'd never been like this. She should've dated a guy from a sex club years ago because Harker definitely knew some tricks that her other boyfriends should've learned. She traced her fingers along the line where the blankets covered his hips.

"I hope you plan on doing something besides staring." His voice was gruff from sleep or maybe desire.

"I thought you were sleeping." Her eyes met his as she continued to run her fingers along his skin.

"I was."

"Sorry. I didn't mean to wake you."

"Don't be sorry for that." He captured her hand and raised it to his mouth, kissing her palm. "You can wake me anytime, but next time do it with your mouth around my dick."

"Oh, wow." She laughed. "Don't hold back. Tell me what you really want."

"And yet, you're still talking." His lips tipped upward in that smirk she used to hate.

"Is this your way of shutting me up." Her hand slid beneath the blankets and grabbed his cock.

"Now, there's an idea." He pushed the covers down, his eyes on her hand as she stroked him. "From now on, instead of telling you to be quiet, I'll just unzip my pants."

"Oh, I don't think that's a good idea." She squeezed him, loving how his dick grew in her hand.

"It's an excellent idea." He touched her cheek. "I'll even get you some knee pads."

"You're so generous." She kissed his hand and then shifted and bent closer to his cock, letting her breath tease his tip.

"I hate to be a complete jerk but you're still talking."

"I am." She licked the underside of his dick. "And I think I'm going to keep talking." She twirled her tongue around his tip. "It's good for you to wait."

"I've waited enough." His hand cupped the back of her neck, pushing her downward.

"Not even close." She kissed up and down his length. She was so going to torture him with pleasure like he'd done to her. "Didn't you explain to me last night about how waiting increased pleasure?"

"This is why I hate smart women." His hand tightened in her hair and he pushed her a little more firmly toward his cock. "Put me in your mouth."

"Say please." She twirled her tongue over his tip.

"Fuck." He groaned. "Please."

"That wasn't so hard, was it?"

"It was un..."

She lowered her mouth over his cock and sucked. She was really good at this. She'd watched a lot of porn and knew a few tricks. If nothing else, when their marriage ended, she was going to make sure that he remembered her as more than just the mother of his child.

CHAPTER 49: Alison

"Let's sit here." Harker stopped at a large, round sectional couch in the back of the Club. There were tables on each end and a large coffee table in front. If there'd been a TV it would've been like any normal living room—except for the crowd of people and the stages.

Alison sat, tugging on her skirt. This one was tighter than the one she'd worn last night. Her eyes skimmed over Harker's ass as he sat next to her.

"Are you checking out my butt?" he asked.

"I like those jeans." She did. His ass looked great in his dress slacks but something about form fitting blue jeans made her insides melt.

"Enjoy tonight because you won't see me in them again."

"You don't like them? How can you not like jeans? There's nothing more comfortable besides maybe sweatpants." She giggled. "Oh, that's what I'm picking next. I have got to see you in sweatpants."

"I wear sweats."

"You do not."

"I do."

"When?"

"When I work out."

"When do you work out?" She'd spent almost every waking moment with this man, and she'd never seen him exercise.

"Every morning." His eyes roamed over her body like a warm caress. "Today's workout had been much more pleasurable than most."

"It was nice."

"Nice?" He growled. "It was a hell of a lot better than nice, and you know it."

"What's wrong with nice?" She fought a grin. She'd used that term to rile him. Today had been wonderful. They'd spent most of the day in bed having sex until they passed out and then doing it again. He'd woken her many times with kisses and his cock. It'd been way better than her alarm clock.

"Nothing if you're describing a cup of tea but when you're talking about sex with me then—"

"Hey Harker, can I get either of you something to drink or eat?" A waitress came over, she was cute with short, light reddish-brown hair and a wide smile.

"Hey, Katie." Harker turned toward Alison. "This is Katie and Katie, this is Alison, my wife."

"Hi, Katie." The words came out like a croak and she cleared her throat. It'd been the first time he'd introduced her as his wife. She hadn't expected it. It was true but it was also only temporary.

"Nice to meet you," said Katie.

"You too." Alison's gaze dropped to her leg where Harker's hand now rested possessively on her upper thigh. His long, talented fingers only a flick away from her pussy. She looked back at the waitress as she grabbed his wrist, trying to unobtrusively push his hand closer toward her knee but the damn man tightened his hold on her thigh.

Katie's gaze dropped for a second then lifted, a hint of laughter in her eyes. "Did you want to order something from the kitchen or just drinks?"

"Drinks." Harker captured Alison's hand with his free one and lifted it off his. "Alison, would you like wine or something stronger?"

She wanted to tell him she'd like him to remove his hand from between her legs but instead said, "A wine cooler would be nice. Strawberry if you have it. If not, then something else berry flavored."

"Got it," said Katie.

"And I'll have bourbon on the rocks," said Harker.

"I'll be right back." Katie headed for the bar.

"You"—Harker shifted sideways toward her—"need to relax."

"Relax? How am I supposed to do that with your hand"—she looked down again—"there?"

"Be thankful I'm restraining myself."

"Restraining? Your fingers are barely an inch away from my...pussy." She whispered the last word.

"Yes. A full inch." He kissed her neck. "And if I wasn't restraining myself, I'd be on my knees with my face buried in your pussy. So be thankful."

"Oh..." Mercy. She was going to leave a wet stain on the couch if he kept talking like that. The man had the most talented tongue she'd ever had the pleasure to meet.

"Yes." He smirked. "Oh." He kissed her knuckles and dropped his hold but left his other hand right where it was, waiting hot and heavy on her thigh.

"Harker. Alison." Ethan stopped in front of them.

"Hi." Dang, she still couldn't believe how hot the man was. She'd almost forgotten to breathe when Harker had introduced her to Ethan earlier that day on one of their few trips out of their room. She shifted, trying to dislodge Harker's hand which brought Ethan's attention right where she didn't want it.

"She's having trouble adjusting to the ways of the Club." Harker moved his fingers, bushing against her pussy.

She trembled. That soft touch was like a jolt of electricity and her body wanted more. What had he done to her? She didn't care where they were. She wanted him to touch her again. They'd spent all day in bed having sex and she still wanted more.

"It's only been one night. Give her time." Ethan smiled softly, his eyes dropping back to where Harker's hand rested.

Alison's libido spiked even more. Ethan was gorgeous and staring at her crotch. She tried not to drool because Harker's dark eyes were boring into her and she wouldn't like it if he stared at another woman right in front of her.

"I have the contracts for you to sign," said Ethan. "If you're going to be here for a bit, I can bring them down."

"Maybe we should go to your office." Harker's eyes met Ethan's. "I think Alison could use some more instructions on Club life." Harker's finger slid across her pussy in a slow stroke.

She grasped his wrist but didn't even try to stop him. She wouldn't succeed and she really didn't want him to quit. Her body ignited with each slide of his finger.

"Is she okay with that?" Ethan's face tightened and his blue eyes darkened as he watched Harker stroke her.

"We'll find out. If not, we'll stop."

"Wh-what are you talking about?" Her words came out breathless as her eyes darted between the two men.

"Harker, I think you need to explain before we go to the office." Ethan sat next to her. "We all need to be clear on what's going to happen."

Harker shifted capturing her chin and turning her head toward him. "Would you like to go to Ethan's office?"

"And...and do what?" She was ready to combust. Harker's fingers still danced along her seam, his other hand holding her face and his dark eyes gleaming with heat. It didn't help that Ethan sat so close to her that his warm breath tickled the back of her neck.

"We'll play...a bit"—Harker looked past her at Ethan—"but not much." His eyes met hers again and they were dark and heavy with desire. "Ethan is going to join us."

"Join?" she croaked, her throat suddenly dry. "Like a threesome?" She was pretty sure her heart was going to explode. She couldn't do that. It was wrong but her body purred at the thought of both of these men kissing her and touching her and...

"Not quite. I'll be the only one who fucks you, but Ethan can touch"—Harker's thumb traced her lips—"and kiss."

"Oh...uhm...I don't know...I'm not sure. Won't it bother you...No of course, it won't. Forget I asked. Almost asked. It was silly. You wouldn't be jealous. You wouldn't have mentioned it if you didn't want to do it. You really want to do this? The three of—"

He touched her lips, silencing her. "I think you'll like it and I trust Ethan to go only as far as I allow."

"I'm very good"—Ethan's words filled her ear, slipping into her head—"at helping women adjust to Club life."

"Ah..." She turned and Ethan's sexy mouth was right there, less than an inch from hers. She licked her lower lip and his eyes heated to a dark blue.

He moved forward slowly, giving her plenty of time to stop him. Harker's finger pressed harder against her pussy, rubbing and she gasped. Ethan's mouth came down on hers, his tongue teasing across her lower lip.

She bolted from the couch. "Ah...ah...I have to use the rest room." She couldn't breathe. Two men. Her. It was hot and too much. She almost ran across the Club.

CHAPTER 50: Harker

"I guess she's not quite ready." Harker stared after Alison's retreating form.

"Guess not." Ethan stood. "I'll go get the contracts."

Harker leaned back on the couch. It annoyed him that he was slightly happy that she'd left. Usually, he didn't mind sharing his sub, but Alison was different. She was his wife. He'd never intended to share her but when he'd seen the interest in her eyes as she'd looked at Ethan, he'd thought, why not?

He wanted to teach her about pleasure, and he'd bet money that she'd never had multiple partners. If she had her first threesome with him, he could decide how far the other man would go. Ethan would be the perfect guy for a Devil's Threesome. He never lost control and he was willing to play almost any role, including taking direction from the sub's master.

Harker wasn't sure how far he would've let Ethan go with Alison, but definitely not sex. He needed to know that any child she'd conceive would be his. He also wasn't letting Ethan take her anal cherry. That belonged to him. So, that left her mouth. The thought of her sucking Ethan's dick didn't sit well with him either. Those gorgeous, talented lips were his to fuck. Watching all that porn for instructions had certainly been worth it. She gave head as well as any pro he'd ever had. He grinned at the memory of last night. He'd ravaged her and she'd loved it. She sure as fuck wouldn't laugh now when she thought of him and her doing anything together.

"Hey." Katie stopped at the table and put down their drinks. "Where's Alison?"

"Bathroom. Put the drinks on my tab. How's your sister?"

"Meh...okay. Morning sickness and bitchy but she's healthy."

"That's good. Parents still not talking to her?" He handed her some money for tip.

"No. It's against everything they believe in for her to be unwed and pregnant. I just wish they'd remember that they love her." Katie's eyes filled with tears. "Hopefully, they'll get over their hurt soon"—she forced herself to smile—"but I'm glad you're in a better mood..."

Harker shook his head, but Katie was looking down as she put the money that he'd given her in her till.

"...than the last time I saw you," she continued.

"Oh, when was that?" Alison moved around Katie and sat next to Harker. "He's almost always in a grumpy mood."

"Not when I'm with you." He put his arm around her and moved toward her for a kiss. Distraction was his best bet, but Alison leaned forward and grabbed her drink. Her gaze still on Katie.

"Oh...uhm..." Katie's eyes widened. "Uh...the last time. I don't recall exactly."

Harker winced inwardly. Katie was a sweet woman and lying wasn't her strong suit.

"You don't recall but you remember he was in a bad mood?" Alison's tone was filled with suspicion.

"Ah...yeah. Like you said, he's always grumpy." Katie looked ready to run.

"Katie," Ethan walked up behind her and now she looked like she was going to puke. "I need to see you in my office."

"Don't blame her," said Harker. "She didn't mean anything."

"Didn't mean anything?" Alison stared at him. "What exactly did she not mean?"

"Anything. It was just a comment. It meant nothing." Harker looked past Alison. "Ethan, don't fire her."

"She knows the rules." Ethan handed Harker the contracts. "Sign these and bring them back whenever."

"Ethan. Don't," said Harker. "Katie didn't know Alison was behind her."

"She knows the rules. She shouldn't have said anything unless you brought it up."

"I did. I brought up a conversation we had that night."

"What night?" Alison's eyes darted between the two, not missing a thing. "Oh my god. Adrian was right. You came here on our wedding night."

"Fuck." Harker closed his eyes for one second. He knew from business that everything could go to shit over one tiny detail; he just hadn't realized it could happen in his personal life too.

Find out what happens next when you read, **Making the Baby** (The Billionaire's Baby book 2)

https://books2read.com/makingthebaby
Or save some money and buy the boxset.
https://books2read.com/thebillionairesbaby

Thanks for reading **The Baby Bargain** *(The Billionaire's Baby series book 1).*

Keep reading for an excerpt of book 2, Making the Baby.

Making the Baby

Harker escorted Alison to their room. He'd won the first battle. She was at the proverbial table and ready to listen. Now, he needed to tell her the truth in a way she wanted to hear. He opened the door.

As soon as she stepped inside, she spun around. "Did you come here on our wedding night?"

"Yes." He closed the door behind him but didn't move. He wasn't chasing her through the Club again. If she wanted to leave, she'd have to go through him.

"Yes?" Her mouth dropped open.

He took her hand. "Listen to—"

"Don't touch me." She pulled away from him. "How could you? You lied to me."

"I did not lie."

"You...you said you didn't—"

"I never said that." He may have implied it but that was different. He moved closer. He needed to touch her, to remind her how good it was between them.

"You may as well have. It might not have been an actual lie, but the intent was a lie."

"You wouldn't talk to me." His patience was disappearing fast. "You wouldn't let me explain. You were ready to throw this all away over nothing."

"You came to a sex club on our wedding night. That's not nothing."

"What did you want me to do?" This was not his fault.

"Excuse me? What did I want you to do on our wedding night? I don't know." She threw up her arms. "Maybe stay with your new wife."

"My new wife?" His temper blew and he stalked closer to her. "You mean the woman who had to drink every drop of alcohol she could find to let me touch her but that still wasn't enough, was it?"

"I apologized for that." She backed away from him.

"Oh, that makes such a fucking difference. You laughed at me."

"I...I was nervous, and I apologized and..." She paused, her nose wrinkling in thought. "No. You do not get to make this about me. This is about you." She poked his chest. "You're the one who went to a sex club on our wedding night."

"Because my bride didn't want me, and why do you care anyway? This isn't a real marriage. You sure like to remind me of that, and it's not like you love me." Those words tangled in his throat.

"You don't love me either." She backed away another step. "And I know this isn't a real marriage, but we have a contract. We agreed to be monogamous.

"You..." He stopped himself. This wasn't the time to correct her about that.

"Were you ever serious about this or was it all some big joke?"

"A joke? If anyone is playing a joke, it's you." He took another step toward her. "I had to bring my wife to a sex club, so she'd see me as a man."

"I...I knew...I know you're a man." She took another step away from him.

"Really? One with a dick or a man like an uncle or eunuch?"

"I...I...You were my boss."

"That's a fantasy for many women but apparently not you." He stalked her across the room.

"No. I never...I..."

"Yes, I know. You never thought of me as a man." That still ripped through his gut like he'd swallowed acid.

"That's not true."

"Isn't it?" He stopped inches from her when her back hit the wall.

"No," she whispered. "I did at first but then..."

"Yeah, that's right. I yelled. You even made a program to laugh about me behind my back."

"How did—"

"You told me all about it. Another gift from my loving wife on our wedding night."

Buy the second book, **Making the Baby**, here.

https://books2read.com/makingthebaby

Or save some money and buy the boxset.

https://books2read.com/thebillionairesbaby

Do you want to meet more of the gorgeous and kinky men and women of La Petite Mort Club? Then check out the excerpts. There's one for the following books:

The Mistletoe Game: Ellie and Adrian meet at the Club on Christmas Eve and end up playing a kinky game, but can Ellie get over her mistrust of alpha men and see Adrian for the man he is?

His Sub (free ebook) — Terry's a dominant but Maggie's not his usual sub. She's a curvy, single mother of three who needs a dominant's guidance more than any woman he's ever met. However, she insists on fighting him every step of the way..

Interviewing for her Lover (free ebook) — Nick's the consummate playboy. Sarah is looking for a lover for a few nights. They should be perfect for each other and they are. Too perfect. Their chemistry is off-the-charts explosive. Will they be able to walk away after only six nights of fantasies? (this book is the first of their six nights together).

The Voyeur (free ebook)–See how Patrick (Adrian's boss) and Annie meet. She's a maid who likes to watch people having sex at the Club. He's given the job of keeping her out of trouble, but he's the biggest danger to her because no matter how hard he tries, he just can't keep his hands off her.

Plus, if you sign up for my newsletter, you can get the entire Six Nights of Sin series for free (all six nights of Nick and Sarah's contract—every delicious fantasy) as a thank you gift.

Click here to join and get your free book[1].

---

1.   https://ellisoday.com/join-newsletter/

Go to my website or email me for details:
www.EllisODay.com[3]
authorEllisOday@gmail.com

---

2. https://ellisoday.com/join-newsletter/

3. http://www.EllisODay.com

FREE: The Mistletoe Game

"Let me introduce you to…Mistletoe Mary!" Desiree pulled a red sheet off another prop.

Shouts and catcalls from crowd filled the air.

"Oh, wow." She had no words.

A sex doll was handcuffed spread eagle to a stand. The doll had long, black hair, open, red lips, a body that most women would envy, and she was naked—completely—and it looked like there was a hole…"I think she's anatomically correct."

Adrian burst out laughing.

"Dang. I said that out loud?" She cringed as she cast a glance at him, making him laugh harder.

"Yes, you did but I'll have to take your word for Mary's *correctness* because I've never met her. I prefer my partners living." His eyes took a quick trip down her frame, leaving heat in their wake.

"Let's see who goes first." Desiree reached into a red, Santa bag, pulling out a chip. She held it up. "Green! Green goes first."

"And my night keeps getting better and better," she mumbled.

"At least it'll be over soon."

"Not soon enough."

"Both of you, come here." Desiree removed another sheet, uncovering a cart filled with twelve glasses each containing a liquid of a different color.

Adrian waved his hand. "Ladies first."

"Chicken," she muttered, his smile making her want to grin as she walked across the stage.

"Stop right there." Desiree pointed at the white line of tape on the floor.

Ellie and Adrian stopped.

Desiree rolled the cart until it was directly to Adrian's right. "I'm sure everyone knows that people kiss under the mistletoe, but the tradition began with a girl standing under the mistletoe. The boys would line up for a kiss, but kisses were limited to the number of berries. They'd wait in line. When they got to the girl, if there was still a berry on the plant, they'd pick it and then kiss her. As soon as the berries were gone, so were the kisses." Desiree paused. "The Mistletoe Game is based on this but"—she stressed the word—"it's been modified in La Petite Mort Club style."

The crowd cheered.

"Adrian, dip the berry into the green glass and then throw it at Mistletoe Mary but be careful where you hit her. Wherever that berry lands is where you get to kiss Ellie and you only get as many kisses as berries."

"Kiss the doll," yelled Marc. "She'll be more fun."

Ellie flipped him the bird because she couldn't pull her eyes from that naked doll. If he hit her breast or...lower...Oh God, she couldn't do this.

"This is getting interesting," said Adrian.

"That isn't the word I'd use," she almost hissed. as she pulled her eyes away from the naked doll. She wanted to slap that sexy smirk off his face but that'd be childish so instead, she grabbed his arm. "Aim for her mouth."

"Her mouth ?" He frowned down at her. "Why would I do that?"

"A kiss. You wanted six kisses."

"And I'm going to get them." His smile was beyond wicked. "All six kisses...wherever I want on your body."

Grab your copy and find out what happens next.

https://books2read.com/mistletoegame

Free - His Sub

Terry wandered through the crowd of well-dressed women and men at La Petite Mort Club. It was the same scene every time Ethan, his friend and owner of the Club, threw one of these events. The members mingled with the newbies, hoping to snag something different or someone interesting.

Ethan strolled casually toward him, a ready smile on his face as he greeted his guests. "Terry, about time you made it down here."

"Like you can talk." His friend spent most of his time in the back office, watching the Club on monitors.

"I've been mingling for over an hour."

"It's your business not mine." He leaned against the balustrade, peering down on the crowd.

"True, but you could sell your practice and buy me out."

"And run this place?" He laughed. "No thank you." He tossed back his scotch. "I spend enough time here as it is." He used to practically live here except when he was at the office or in court, but lately he'd been staying home more.

"Good turn out tonight." Ethan waved at a waitress and a moment later they each had another drink.

"Yeah, but I don't see one interesting person in this crop of wannabe members."

"And you can tell if someone is interesting just by looking at them?"

"I can tell not one of them has an original thought. Look at them. They're all in red." The Club was awash in a sea of red dresses—short, long, dark, light but always red.

"It is a Valentine's Day party."

"I know but you'd think one woman"—he held up his finger—"one would consider that everyone else would be in red and wear a different color."

"There are some pinks out there."

"Same thing, just lighter."

Ethan grabbed his phone from his pocket and looked at the text, frowning.

"Problem?" The Club was usually a safe place but on open night events, when Ethan allowed non-members access in order to recruit new members, the place could get dangerous.

"A little skirmish over a woman." Ethan grinned, his blue eyes sparkling as a couple of young guys hurried past them, almost tripping in their haste to stay close to a group of very attractive women. "These youngsters haven't learned that sharing is more fun."

He ignored Ethan's teasing. He'd taken a lot of shit from Ethan, Nick and even Patrick because he wasn't into the sharing thing. He preferred it to be him and one woman, one sweet, little sub. Since he was in no mood to listen to any more crap, he'd change the subject. "Those kids barely look old enough to drink."

"You're showing your age." Ethan patted his shoulder. "You should find some nice, young thing and teach her how to please her master."

"Maybe I will, if any of them show enough originality to dress in something other than red."

"I've got to go and sort out this problem." Ethan slid his phone into his pocket. "I'll find you later. If you find that elusive non-red dress, I'd suggest we share but..." He chuckled as he headed down the stairs, maneuvering through the crowd like he had nowhere to go, when in reality he was heading for the back—the playrooms.

Terry's eyes stopped and lingered on the new hire, Desiree, who was moving around the room, talking and flirting with all the men and some women. She was interesting—exotic and smart—but there was a shrewdness behind her eyes that he'd learned a long time ago to avoid. A woman like her had an agenda and she stuck with it, no matter what.

Someone slammed into his back, causing his drink to spill down his front, staining his shirt and suit.

"Oh...oh, I'm so sorry."

He spun around and encountered a red dress and breasts—milky white and lush. The skin would be fragrant and softer than rose petals.

"Oh. Your shirt. Let me get something to wipe that up."

He forced his eyes away from those lovely breasts. Her hair was a rich mahogany. It'd probably hang past her shoulders in waves of curly silk but right now it was piled haphazardly on her head in what had been some kind of elegant style before disobedient strands had escaped their restraint. She looked mussed and damnit, he wanted to be the one to muss her.

"Paper towels? Napkins?" She glanced around and then hurried over to the bar.

She was short and curvy—her body succulent, ripe and he'd bet juicy. She grabbed a stack of napkins and headed for him. Her dress was too tight, like she'd recently gained some weight. He usually went for the tall, athletic types but for some reason his dick had picked this woman.

She returned to his side and dabbed at the wetness on his shirt and jacket as if she actually gave a shit about his clothes. This was no subtle caress, no flirtation—just indifferent efficiency.

"I'm so sorry." She wadded the napkins in her hand, still patting at his clothes.

"You said that already." His words came out gruffer than he'd meant. No one treated him with disinterest. He was a rich, successful, attractive man and she was treating him like a child. He wanted to pull up her—unfortunately, red—dress and fuck her right here. They were at the Club. It wasn't out of the question.

Her hand froze. "Oh." Her large hazel eyes looked startled and then hurt. "Sorry. Ah, excuse me." She headed toward the stairs, dropping the wet napkins in the trash before disappearing in the crowd.

He turned around, so he could see the first floor and waited for her to appear. She hurried across the downstairs room, bumping and stumbling through the crowd. A lone, scared, little rabbit in a room full of predators. She stopped for a moment, scanning the crowd as if searching for someone.

"Who are you looking for, little rabbit?" he mumbled to himself. "A husband? Boyfriend?" He grinned as he lifted his scotch to his lips. "Girlfriend?" He frowned at the empty glass. "You spilled my drink. I'll forgive you, but it's going to cost you." He waved at one of the waitresses. "Everything has a price, little rabbit." As one of the best divorce lawyers in town, he knew that better than anyone.

The waitress brought him another drink. He paid, giving her a large tip before turning to find his little rabbit. He took a sip of the scotch, enjoying the smooth burn and his lush little bunny's journey through La Petite Mort Club. She froze in her tracks, her jaw dropping open as she gazed at a threesome on one of the couches.

The woman was sandwiched between two men, stroking one's cock as the other man fondled her beneath her red dress. The man behind her looked up and said something to the little rabbit. Her face heated and Terry's eyes dropped to her chest. Yep, they were a pretty shade of pink but what he really wanted to know was if the color matched her pussy.

She stumbled away from the threesome, bumping into another man. It was Richard, who stopped her from falling and then immediately let her go, stepping away. She was safe with Richard. As a member of the Club and a gentleman, he knew that safewords were law and consent was absolutely necessary. She said something to Richard and continued through the Club, disappearing in the crowd.

"You're not getting away that easily." He followed along on the upper floor, keeping her in sight. He had no idea why but he wanted her. Maybe it was simply because she was different than everyone else here.

He took another sip of his drink. It was obviously the little rabbit's first time at a place like this but she didn't seem eager to participate or interested in watching. She truly seemed to be looking for someone specific—not just someone to fuck. Well, she'd found the latter because he was going to fuck her. In the office he followed his head but at La Petite Mort Club his cock was king.

She headed toward the playrooms. There was no way he was going to miss this. He sauntered down the stairs, grabbing another drink on the way. She wasn't hard to follow. She left a path of irritated people in her wake as she bumped into them and apologized profusely before hurrying forward. Her full, round hips swayed under her tight, red dress that'd seen better days—hem frayed and at least five years out of style. Not that he minded, especially the snug fit of the cloth, but his women were usually much more put tougher.

They were the CEO types—women who thrived on being in charge. He enjoyed teaching them how much fun turning over control could be. When they were with him, he was their dom, their master and he made sure they loved every second. He told them when to kneel, when to suck, when to spread their legs or ass and when to come. The more power they had in their everyday life the more they craved bowing to his wishes. His little rabbit wouldn't know what power was. She was a hot mess of a woman. Still, his dick wanted her, so his dick would have her.

She was hurrying out of the first playroom when he entered the hallway. Her eyes were huge and her cheeks were on fire. She ducked into the next room and quickly came out—even redder than before.

"Excuse me." He'd offer his assistance in her search. She'd be grateful. He could capitalize on that unless she was looking for her husband or boyfriend. He wasn't in the mood to share. He would, however, allow the other man to watch. He could give the guy some pointers on how to take care of his wife because this woman obviously needed guidance.

"You?" Her eyes narrowed.

That wasn't the reaction he was used to. Women usually purred for him.

"Are you following me?"

"What would you do if I said I was?" He took a step toward her.

"I'd scream. There are bouncers here. I saw them."

Lord, she was cute. "Yes, but if they came running at every little scream they'd die of exhaustion."

As if to emphasis his point a woman screamed in ecstasy. His little rabbit's face heated and she averted her gaze.

"Who are you looking for?" He ran his finger lightly down her cheek. Her skin was as smooth as porcelain but much warmer and softer.

"Ah..." Her breath hitched, making her breasts swell dangerously above her gown.

He could have her out of it in a minute. The skin would be even softer than that on her face. "Did you lose your husband?"

"No." She licked her lips.

There was no way he could let that offer pass. He slowly bent, giving her time to refuse him. He may command his women but he made sure they always wanted it first. Her eyes dropped to his mouth and he couldn't help a slight smirk. She wanted this as much as he did. He moved closer and let his lips rest gently on hers. He'd take it slow, make her yearn for him and then he'd make her obey.

"What are you doing?" She turned her head.

"Kissing you." His lips brushed against her cheek. He wasn't about to lose ground.

"Why?" She turned again, her eyes meeting his.

The confusion in her hazel gaze was as obvious as the hideous dress on her gorgeous body. She may remind him of a rabbit but she couldn't be that naive. She had to be in her mid to late thirties.

He should use flowery words—tell her she was beautiful, desirable—but that wasn't him. Blunt was the kindest word to describe him. "Because, I want to."

"You don't even know me."

He was losing ground. The interest in her face was being replaced with disgust. "No, but I know I want you." Damn, he shouldn't have said that.

"Well, too bad." She pushed on his chest and he stepped back, letting her pass.

"This is a sex club, you know." He followed. "If you aren't here for sex, why are you here?"

She spun around. "I'm quite aware of what this place is and just because I don't want you, a stranger to...to"—she waved her hand about—"in the hallway."

He laughed. "We wouldn't be the first. There are people fucking in the main room."

"I know. I saw." Her cheeks heated.

He stepped closer. "You are adorable." He touched a strand of hair that was resting on her shoulder. It was like satin.

"I'm a mess." She pulled her hair free from his fingers.

"A hot mess. A fiery, hot, sexy mess." He moved closer with every other word. "One I want to fuck, right now."

Her eyes hardened. "Too bad because I don't"—again she waved her hand about—"you know, with strangers in the hallway." She shoved his chest again.

He took a small step back but he wasn't giving up yet. "We can go to a private room."

"No."

Shit. By the look on her face, he'd just made a bigger blunder.

"Let me go." She pushed him again.

Damn. She'd said the worst three words in the English language besides I love you. He moved away, releasing her for the moment. "Sorry."

She harrumphed.

"I made a mistake."

"Yes, you did." She hurried down the hallway but not before he'd seen the look of hurt in her large eyes.

"What the fuck do you want from me? I made a mistake and apologized." He trailed after her.

"I want you to leave me alone. Please. Go away."

He stopped. His little rabbit was running but perhaps, he shouldn't chase. She darted down a hallway toward the hardcore BDSM rooms.

Normally, she'd be fine—embarrassed but fine. Except with all the newbies here, tonight wasn't a normal night. He hurried after her. "Hey, I don't think you want to go—"

"Leave me alone." She walked faster. "I need to find my friend and get out of here."

"Okay, but I don't—"

"Go away." She sounded both mad and as if she were going to cry.

"Suit yourself, but I warned you."

She strode into the closest room. He should leave. Let her find out that he wasn't the worst thing in a place like this, not in a long shot, but his feet followed her. She was his little rabbit. He'd found her. No one else was going to enjoy her until he'd had his taste.

"Vicky? Vicky? Are you in here?"

He stepped into the room, staying in the shadows. She was looking around in the dark for her friend. It only took a moment for one of the six guys to notice the little rabbit who'd stumbled into their den.

"Shit," he mumbled. Not one of those guys was a regular.

<u>Grab your free copy and find out what happens next.</u>[1]

---

1. https://books2read.com/u/3yrBlV

Free: Interviewing For Her Lover

"Do I have to take off my clothes?" Sarah tugged on the hem of her black dress. It was shorter and lower cut in the front than she normally wore, but the Viewing was about finding a man for sex and according to Ethan men liked to look.

"No." Ethan turned her away from the door and forced her to look at him. "You don't have to do anything you don't want to do."

She stared into his blue eyes. Why couldn't he be interested in her? She'd only met with him five or six times, but she trusted him. He ran his business, La Petite Mort Club, very professionally and he was gorgeous with his sandy brown hair, strong cheekbones and vibrant blue eyes. Sex between them would be good. Easy. He was attractive and...not for her. She didn't want decent sex or good sex, she wanted mind blowing, screaming orgasms and that wouldn't happen between him and her because there was no chemistry, no attraction.

"Listen to me." He moved his hands to her shoulders and gave her a gentle shake. "You aren't selling yourself to the highest bidder. You're looking for a partner. One who'll"—he grinned—"turn you on in ways you can't even imagine."

She glanced at the door where the men waited. Waited for her. Waited to decide if they wanted to fuck her. "I'm a bit nervous."

"About what?"

This was embarrassing, but she'd been honest with him up to this point. She'd had to be. He was helping her...had helped her to choose the five men in the other room. "What if none of them..."

"They will want you." He touched her chin, turning her face toward him. "A few of them may back out after this but not because they don't want you."

"Yeah, right."

"I'm only going to say this once. You're beautiful and different, unique."

"That's not necessarily a good thing." She had long legs and a nice body—trim and firm—but with her auburn hair and green eyes she was cute at best, not gorgeous. The men she'd chosen were all rich, good looking and powerful. They could have anyone they wanted.

"It's exactly what they want, or most of them anyway." He took her hand and led her closer to the door.

She leaned on his arm, hating these shoes. She should've stuck with her flats but Ethan had given her a list of what she should wear and high heels were on the top. She'd found the smallest heels in the store and by Ethan's look when he'd first seen her she might've been better off going barefoot. He'd met her at the private entrance and his gaze had been appreciating as it'd skimmed over her dress until he got to her feet. Then he'd frowned and shook his head.

"Finding the right men for you wasn't easy." He stopped at the door.

"Thanks a lot." She shifted away from him, his words hurting a little. She hadn't been sure of her appeal to the opposite sex in a long time, not since the early years with Adam.

"It's not because you aren't beautiful but because you want to be dominated and you want to dominate—"

"I do not want to dominate." All she could picture was a woman in black leather with a whip and that wasn't her, not at all.

"If you say so." He smiled a little. "But, you do want to lead the scene. Right? Because that's what—"

"Yes." Her face was red. She could feel it. She didn't want to talk about her fantasies again. It'd been embarrassing enough the first time, but he'd had to know what she wanted to compile a list of candidates.

"Most at the club are either doms or subs. Very few are switches." His eyes raked over her. "That's what's so special about you. You want it all and...that's what made choosing these men difficult."

He'd given her a selection of twenty-two men who might be interested in what she wanted. She'd narrowed it down to seven. Two had been uninterested when he'd approached. That'd left her with the five who'd see her in person for the first time tonight, but she wouldn't see them. That'd come after the Viewing when she interviewed any who were still interested.

"Remember what you want. This is your deal. You call the shots. At least a little." He kissed her forehead. "But don't refuse to give them anything. You don't want a submissive."

"No." That didn't turn her on at all and she only had eight weeks. One night each week for two months before she'd go back to her lonely life, her lonely bed, dreaming of Adam.

"You can do this." He pulled a flask from his jacket and unscrewed the lid. "For courage."

"Thanks." She took a large swallow, the brandy too thick and sweet for her taste but it was better than nothing.

"Now, go find your lover."

She laughed a little but sadness swept through her. There'd be no love between this man and herself. This would be sex, fucking. That's all. The only man she'd ever love, her only lover, was dead. This was purely physical. "Thank you again." She stood on tip-toe and kissed his cheek. He may be gorgeous and run a sex club but he was a good man, a good friend.

She turned and opened the door and walked into the room, trying to stay balanced on these stupid heels. Men wouldn't find them so attractive if they had to wear them. The room was dark except for one light highlighting a small platform. That was for her. She stepped up onto the small stage. The room was silent but they were there, above her, hidden behind the one-way mirrors, watching and deciding if they wanted to take the next step—to eventually take her.

She stared into the blackness of the room. It wasn't huge but its emptiness made it seem vast. She glanced upward, the light making her squint and she quickly stared back into the darkness. This was arranged for them to see her. That was it. She'd get no glimpse of them yet. She'd seen their pictures, chosen them but meeting them in person would be different. A picture couldn't tell her their smell or the sound of their voices.

She tugged at her dress where it hugged her hips, wishing the questions would start, but there was only silence. She shifted, the heels already killing her feet. Ethan hadn't liked them and if they weren't going to impress, she might as well take them off. She moved to the back of the stage, leaned against the wall and removed her shoes. As she returned to the center of the stage a man spoke, his voice loud and commanding almost echoing throughout the room.

"Don't stop there. Take off your dress."

She bent, placing her shoes on the floor. That wasn't part of the deal. She wasn't going to undress in front of five men, only one. Only the one she chose. She straightened. "No."

"What?" He was surprised and not happy.

"I said no. That's not part of the Viewing."

"I want to see what I'm getting."

She stared up toward the windows, squinting a little. She couldn't tell from where the voice had come. The speaker system made it sound as if it were coming from God himself. "And you will if I pick you."

Another man laughed.

"It's not funny. She's disobedient," said the man with the loud voice.

"Not always. I can be obedient." These men liked to be in control but sometimes, so did she.

"Will you raise your dress? Just a little," asked another voice.

"Didn't you see enough in the photos?" She'd applied a few months ago for this one-time contract. She'd been excited and nervous when she'd received the acceptance email with an appointment for a photography session. She'd never had her picture professionally taken, since she didn't count school portraits or the ones her parents had had done at JCPenny's. She'd been anxious and a little turned on imaging wearing her new lingerie in front of a strange man, so she'd been disappointed to find the photographer was an elderly woman, but the lady had put her at ease and the photos had turned out better than she'd expected. She glanced up at the mirrors, hoping she wasn't disappointing all the men. That'd be too embarrassing.

"Those were...nice, but I'd like to see the real thing before deciding if you're worth my time."

She raised a brow. "You can always leave." She shouldn't antagonize him. She was sure the bossy man had already decided against committing to this agreement. Disobedience didn't appeal to him. That left four. If she didn't pick any of them, she could go through the process again, but she didn't think she would.

The man chuckled slightly. "I know that, but I haven't decided I don't want to fuck you. Not yet, anyway."

The word, so harsh and vulgar excited her. It was the truth. That was what she, what they were all deciding. Who'd get to fuck her. It was what she wanted, what she'd agreed to do, and as much as she dreaded it, she wanted it. She was tired of being alone. She missed having a man inside her—his tongue and fingers and cock.

"Do any of you have any questions?" She clasped her dress at her waist and slowly gathered it upward, displaying more and more of her long legs. She ran. They were in shape. The men would like them.

"Lower your top," said the same man who'd told her to take off her dress.

She didn't like him. If he didn't back out, she'd have Ethan remove him from her list. He was too commanding. He'd never allow her to be in control.

"I don't know if he's done looking at my legs yet." She continued raising the dress until her black and green lace panties were almost exposed.

"Very nice and thank you," said the polite man.

"You're welcome." This man might work. She shifted the dress up another inch before dropping it, giving them a glance at her panties.

"Now, your top," said the bossy guy.

She lowered her spaghetti string off one shoulder, letting the dress dip, but not enough to show anything besides the side of her bra.

"More," he said.

"No." She raised the strap, covering herself. She didn't like this man and wished he'd leave. She'd kick him out but that wasn't part of the process and they were very firm about their rules at this club.

"He got to see your pussy. Why don't I get to see your tits?"

"You got to see as much as he did." She was ready to move on. She bent and picked up her shoes. "If there's nothing else, gentleman, we can set up times for the interview process."

"Turn around," said another man.

It was a command, but she didn't mind. There was a politeness to his order and something about the texture of his voice caused an ache between her thighs. There was a caress in his tone but with an edge and a promise of a good hard fuck.

"Are you going to obey?" His words were whisper soft and smooth.

"Yes." That was going to be part of this too. Her commanding and him commanding. She dropped her shoes and turned.

"Raise you dress again."

She looked over her shoulder at where she imagined he sat watching her.

"Please." There was humor in his tone.

She smiled and slowly gathered the dress upward. She stopped right below the curve of her bottom.

"More. Please." There was a little less humor in his voice.

She wanted to show him her ass. She wanted to show that voice everything but not with the others around. This would be just her and one man, one stranger. That was one of her rules. "No. Only if you're picked do you get to see any more of me than you have." She dropped her dress, grabbed her shoes and walked off the stage and out the door.

She was going to have sex with a stranger. She was going to live out her fantasies for eight nights with a man she didn't know and would never really know, but she wasn't going to lose who she was. She'd keep her honor and her dignity which meant she had to pick a man who'd agree with her rules.

Get your free copy and find out what happens next.
https://books2read.com/u/3nYKo6

Free: The Voyeur

Annie finished making the bed and gathered the sheets from the floor, keeping them as far away from her body as possible. These sex rooms were disgusting and Ethan was a jerk making her work as a maid. She almost had her Bachelor's Degree in Culinary Arts, but he'd refused to hire her for the kitchen—too many men in the kitchen. The only job he'd give her at La Petite Mort Club was as a maid and unfortunately, she needed the money too badly to refuse.

She stuffed the dirty sheets into the cart and hurried out the door. She had almost thirty minutes before she had to be at the next "sex room." She hid the cart in a closet and darted down a back hallway, staying clear of the cameras. Julie, the woman who supervised the daytime maids, was a real bitch. If she were caught sneaking away from her duties, she'd be assigned to the orgy rooms every day. Right now, they all took turns cleaning that nightmare. She swore they should get hazard pay to even go in those rooms.

She slipped through a doorway and hurried to the one-way mirror. She stared at the couple in the next room. From her first day here, she'd been curious about the activities at the club. She was twenty-four and wasn't a virgin but she'd never, ever done some of these things.

The woman in the room below was tied to a table, legs spread and wearing some sort of leather outfit that left her large breasts free and her crotch exposed. She had shaved her pussy and her pink lower lips were swollen and glistening from her excitement. The man strolled around the table as if he had all night. He still had his pants on but had removed his shirt. His arms and chest were well defined but he had a slight paunch. His erection tented his pants and Annie felt wetness pool between her legs. She had no idea why watching this turned her on but it did. Ever since she'd accidentally barged in on that guy and girl in the Interview room, she couldn't stop watching.

The man below ran his hand up the woman's inner thigh, glancing over her pussy. The woman thrust her hips upward and Annie ran her own hand between her legs. The man's mouth moved but Annie couldn't hear anything and then he slapped the woman across the thigh hard enough to leave a red mark. Annie jumped. She wasn't into that, but she couldn't stop watching the woman's face. At first, it'd contorted in pain but then it'd morphed into pleasure. The man hit her again and then bent, kissing the red welts—running his tongue across them as his fingers squeezed her nipple.

Annie clutched her thighs together, searching for some relief. Her panties were soaked. It wouldn't take but a few strokes to make her come. She started to slide her hand into her pants.

"Having fun?" asked a deep voice from behind her.

She spun around, her heart dropping into her stomach. "Ah...I was just finishing cleaning in here." Damn, she should've closed the door but she hadn't expected anyone in this area. The rooms were off limits on this floor until tonight and she was the only one assigned to clean here.

He shut the door and locked it before strolling toward her. She'd seen him around the Club, but more than that she remembered him from the military photos her brother, Vic, had sent to her. She carried one of the three of them—Vic, Ethan and this guy, Patrick—in her purse. He'd been attractive in the picture, but now that he was older and in person he was gorgeous. He had dark green eyes, brown hair and a perfect body. He stopped so close to her his chest almost brushed against her breasts. She was pretty sure it would if she inhaled deeply. She really wanted to take that deep breath and feel his hard chest against her breasts.

"Don't let me stop you from enjoying the show."

"I...I wasn't. I should go." She started to walk past him but he grabbed her hand.

His grip was warm and strong but loose enough that she could pull free if she wanted. She didn't. Even though she only knew him from her brother's pictures and letters, she'd had many fantasies about him when she'd been in high school. Her gaze dropped to the front of his pants and her mouth almost watered. He was definitely interested. She dragged her eyes up his body, stopping on his face. He smiled at her.

"There's nothing to be embarrassed about. Watching turns us all on." He kissed the back of her hand and she jumped as his tongue darted out, tasting her skin.

"I...I should go." She didn't move.

"No, you should watch." He dropped her hand and grabbed her shoulders, gently turning her toward the mirror. He trailed his hands up and down her arms. "Watch."

The man in the other room was now sucking on the woman's breast as his fingers caressed her pussy.

"Would you like to hear them? Or do you like it quiet?" His voice was a rough whisper against her ear.

"Sound, please." She wanted to hear their gasps and moans. She wanted to close her eyes and pretend it was her. She shifted, squeezing her thighs together.

He chuckled as he moved away. She felt his absence to her bones. He'd been strong and warm behind her and for a moment she'd felt safe, safer than she had since her brother had come back from the war, broken and sad, and her father had started drinking again.

The woman's moans filled the room and Patrick came back to stand behind her, this time placing his hands on her waist.

"I'm Patrick," he said against her ear.

She couldn't take her eyes from the scene in front of her. The woman was almost coming as the man thrust his fingers inside of her.

"What's your name?" He nipped her neck and she jumped.

"I...I..." If she told him her name, he might say something to Ethan. Ethan would kill her if he knew she was in here watching.

"Tell me your name." His lips trailed along her neck and she tipped her head giving him better access.

The guy was kissing his way down the woman's body. Annie wanted to touch herself, to make herself come but Patrick was here.

He nibbled her ear. "Why won't you tell me your name?"

"I...I'll get in trouble." She rubbed her ass against his erection, hopefully giving him a hint.

"Tease." His hand drifted down her stomach, stopping right above where she wanted him to touch. "Tell me your name or I'll make you suffer." He unbuttoned her pants and left his hand—warm, rough but immobile—resting on her abdomen.

"I can't." She stood on tip-toe, hoping his hand would lower a little but he was too tall or she was too short. He had to be almost six foot and she was barely five-foot four. "I could get fired and I need this job."

"Darling, Ethan won't fire you for fucking a customer."

"We can't." She spun around. She hadn't thought this through. He was her fantasy come to life and she wanted him to be hers just for a moment, but Ethan would find out and then she'd be in deep shit.

"Don't worry. I'm a member and you work here, so we're both clean." He hesitated, his hands tightening on her hips. "Are you protected?"

"What?" She had no idea what he was talking about.

"Ethan makes sure everyone at the Club is clean but only the...some of his employees are required to be on birth control." He ran his hands up her sides, getting closer and closer to her breasts. "Are you on birth control?" His eyes darkened as they dropped to her tits. "If not, it's okay. There are other things we can do."

Oh, she wanted to do everything his eyes promised, but she couldn't. "No, I'll get in trouble. I need this job. I have to go." She tried to move but her feet refused to obey, so she just stared at his handsome face.

"Are you sure?" He bent so he was almost eye level with her. "I promise. Ethan won't care. A lot of maids become...change jobs. The pay's a lot better." His eyes roamed over her frame. "Especially, for someone as cute as you."

Ethan would kill her before letting her become one of his pleasure associates.

"I could talk to Ethan for you." His hands moved up her body, stopping right below her breasts.

Her nipples hardened and she forgot everything but what he was making her feel. He ran his thumb over one of them and she leaned closer, wanting him to do it again.

He did. He continued rubbing her nipple as he spoke. "I could persuade him to let me...handle your initiation into club life."

Her heart raced in her chest. It could be just her and him doing all these things she'd seen. Her pussy throbbed but she couldn't do it. She wouldn't do it. She couldn't have sex for money. Her parents were both dead but they'd never understand and she couldn't disappoint them. "No. I can't do that...not for money." Her eyes darted to the door. She needed to get out of there before she did something she'd regret.

"That's even better." He smiled as he stepped closer. "We can keep this between us. No money. Only a man and a woman." He leaned down and whispered in her ear, "Giving each other pleasure. A lot of pleasure. In ways you haven't even imagined."

There were moans from the other room and she glanced over her shoulder. The man's face was buried between the woman's thighs.

Patrick turned her around, pulling her against him and wrapping his arms around her waist. "Are you wet?"

"What? No." She struggled in his arms, her ass brushing against his erection again.

"Oh fuck. Do that again." He kissed her neck, open mouthed and hot.

She stopped trying to get away. She wanted this...this moment. She shouldn't but she did, so she wiggled her butt against him again. He was hard and long and her body ached for him. It'd been too long she'd had sex. She needed this.

"Would you like me to touch you?" His hands drifted over her hips and down her thighs.

She'd like him to do all sorts of things to her. She nodded.

"Say it." His words were a command she couldn't disobey.

"Yes."

"Yes, what?" He untucked her shirt from her pants.

"Touch me. Please." She was already pushing her hips toward his hand. She wanted his hand on her, his fingers inside of her.

"Are you wet?" he asked again.

She inhaled sharply as he unzipped her pants.

"Don't lie to me. I'll find out in a minute."

She'd never talked dirty during sex and she wasn't sure she was ready to do that with a stranger. Her heart skipped a beat. Maybe, she shouldn't be doing any of this with a stranger. She grabbed his hand. "Maybe, we shouldn't."

The woman below cried out and the man straightened, wiping his face and unbuttoning his pants.

"Watch. The main event is about to happen." Patrick's hot breath tickled her neck.

Her gaze locked on the man's penis. It was large and demanding. He straddled the woman, grabbing his cock.

"Don't you want to feel some of what they feel?" He nibbled on her ear and then neck. "I can help you."

She may not know him, but she trusted him. He was a former marine. He'd been a good friend of Vic's. He wouldn't hurt her and she needed to come. She loosened her grip, letting go of his hand. He slipped inside her pants, caressing her pussy through her underwear. His fingers were long and strong. She closed her eyes, leaning against him as he stroked her.

"You're already so wet and hot." His breath was a warm caress on her ear. "But, I'm going to make you wetter and then, I'm going to make you come." His other hand shoved her pants down, giving him more room to work. "Open your eyes and watch the show."

She did as he said. The man was inside the woman, thrusting hard and fast. The woman was moaning and trying to move but the restraints kept her mostly helpless.

"Fuck, you're soaked." Patrick's hand cupped her and she arched into his touch, rubbing her ass against his erection. He shoved his hand inside her underwear, his finger running along her folds until he slipped one inside.

"Oh." She grabbed his hand—not to push him away, but to make sure he didn't leave.

He smiled against her hair. "Don't worry, baby. I won't stop." He stroked his finger inside of her and his wrist brushed against her clit.

She needed more. She needed to touch him, feel him. She turned her head, wrapping her arms up and around his neck. He kissed her. It was desperate and wild, but he stopped too soon.

"They're almost done. You don't want to miss it."

She turned back to the mirror. The man below continued to fuck the woman as Patrick finger-fucked her. His other hand slipped under her shirt to her breast. His lips sucked her neck as he rocked his erection against her ass. He was everywhere, and she was so close. The muscles in her legs constricted. Her hips tipped upward.

"Wait, baby," he groaned in her ear, as he pushed a second finger inside of her. "Just a few more minutes."

His fingers were stretching her and it felt wonderful. She moaned, long and low as he thrust harder and faster, almost matching the pace of the man in the other room. She could almost imagine it was Patrick's cock and not his fingers inside of her.

"Oh…oh," she cried out. He was pushing her toward the edge. Her body was spiraling with each pump of his fingers. She was going to come—right here while watching that couple. It was so dirty and so wrong and it only made her hotter.

The woman below screamed and her body stiffened. The man thrust again and again and then grunted his release.

"Show's over." Patrick nipped her neck at the same time he pressed down on her clit with his thumb, sending her shooting into her orgasm.

She trembled and he pulled her close, his hand still cupping her pussy and his fingers still inside of her. When her heartbeat had settled, he removed his hand and bent, pulling off her shoes and removing her pants before lifting her and carrying her to the wall.

"My turn." He wrapped her legs around his waist.

Her phone rang. "My work phone. I...I have to answer it."

"When we're done." He unzipped his pants.

"Annie, answer the phone. I know you're around here. I can hear it ringing you stupid bitch," yelled Julie.

"Oh, shit." She shoved Patrick away, and ran across the room, grabbing her clothes off the floor. "It's my boss. She'll kill me if she finds me like this."

"I'll take care of Julie." He headed for the door, zipping up his fly. "Don't move." He grinned over his shoulder at her. "You can take off your pants again, but other than that, don't move."

"No. Please." She raced over to him, grabbing his arm. "I need this job." And Ethan could not find out about this.

"She won't fire you. She can't. Only Ethan can fire you." He bent and kissed her.

His lips were gentle and coaxing this time and her body swayed into him. He pulled her even closer and she could feel his cock, thick and heavy, pushing against her. Her pussy tightened again in anticipation.

"Damn it, Annie. This is going to be so much worse if I have to call your stupid phone again. Get out here!" Julie was only a few doors down.

She grabbed Patrick and tugged on his hand. "Please, hide." She glanced around, looking for somewhere that would conceal a six-foot muscular man.

"I'm not going to hide from Julie."

Get Your FREE Copy and find out what happens next
https://books2read.com/u/bxqBMk

COMING SOON:

ETHAN'S STORY
MATTIE'S STORY
JAKE'S STORY
REBECCA AND DEREK'S STORY
VIC'S STORY

Email me with questions, concerns or to let me know what you thought of the book. I love hearing from readers.
authorEllisODay@gmail.com

https://www.EllisODay.com
Follow me
Facebook
https://www.facebook.com/EllisODayRomanceAuthor/
Closed FB Group (sneak peeks, sample chapters, and other bonuses)
https://www.facebook.com/groups/153238782143373
Bookbub
https://www.bookbub.com/authors/Ellis-o-day

Instagram
https://www.instagram.com/authorEllisODay/[1]

---

1. https://www.instagram.com/authorellisoday/

Twitter
https://twitter.com/Ellis_o_day

Pinterest
www.pinterest.com\AuthorEllisODay[2]

ABOUT THE AUTHOR

Ellis O. Day loves reading and writing about love and sex. She believes that although the two don't have to go together, it's best when they do (both in life and in fantasy).

Don't miss out!

Visit the website below and you can sign up to receive emails whenever Ellis O. Day publishes a new book. There's no charge and no obligation.

https://books2read.com/r/B-A-WMME-WWZOB

BOOKS 2 READ

Connecting independent readers to independent writers.

Also by Ellis O. Day

Hot Holidays
The Mistletoe Game
A Banging New Year
Cupid's Misfire

La Petite Mort Club
Six Nights of Sin
The Voyeur Series Books 1 - 4
Six Weeks of Seduction
A Merry Masquerade For Christmas
The Dom's Submission Series (Parts 1-3)
Hot Holidays
The Billionaire's Baby

La Petite Mort Club Intimate Encounters
His Lesson
Playing House
His Love
His Imperfect Day

Six Nights Of Sin
Interviewing For Her Lover
Taking Control
School Fantasy
Master-Slave Fantasy
Punishment Fantasy
The Proposition

The Billionaire's Baby
The Baby Bargain
Making the Baby
The Baby Battle
Having The Baby

The Dom's Submission
His Sub
His Mission
His Submission

The Voyeur
The Voyeur
Watching the Voyeur
Touching the Voyeur
Loving the Voyeur